D0457798

The STITCHERS

FRIGHT WATCH

The STITCHeRS

LORIEN LAWRENCE

Amulet Books
New York

Cataloging-in-Publication Data has been applied for
and may be obtained from the Library of Congress.

ISBN 978-1-4197-4692-5

Printed and bound in U.S.A.
10 9 8 7 6 5 4 3 2 1

ABRAMS The Art of Books
195 Broadway, New York, NY 10007
abramsbooks.com

For my dad, whom I miss a little more each day.
Wish he was here to read this.

CHAPTER 1

If there's one thing I know for certain, it's that Mike Warren is always late.

Calm down, he texts. ***I'm coming.***

I sigh heavily as though he can hear me from his house, which almost leans against my own, they're so close together. From the outside, the houses themselves are nearly identical, except there's a dog perched in my living room window. Billy's old eyes stare me down as if to ask, *Why don't you take me with you anymore?* I offer him a weak smile before turning back around, facing Goodie Lane.

"You ready?" Mike asks, startling me as he finally joins me on the sidewalk. He lowers his Yankees hat over his eyes and offers me one of his smirks before flicking on the end of my ponytail.

"Are you *ever* going to be on time?" I ask, tossing my hair out of his reach. "It's six thirty-five."

"Wow, Parker. Five whole minutes."

"Yes: Five. Whole. Minutes. *Late.*"

"What can I say? I need my beauty sleep in the morning. Unlike *some* people." He raises an eyebrow in a way that makes me blush. He notices and laughs. "Just kidding, Parker. Don't be so serious."

I scowl at him and start to jog in place. "You warm?"

"Who isn't? It's ninety degrees out here."

"Then let's go. They're not coming."

"Of course they're coming. They come every morning."

I wave my hand across the street, motioning to the empty lawns. "Look. No one's there."

He whistles under his breath just as one of the front doors opens. "Told you. Here comes Ms. Bea."

I follow his gaze just as our neighbor glides out of her house on a pair of delicate heels. As usual, her face is painted as if she's ready for an old-movie premiere even though it's six thirty in the morning: red lips, rosy cheeks, spider-leg lashes, and smooth, plastic-looking skin despite the fact that she's supposedly older than my grandma Jane. A layered gold necklace hangs around her neck, shimmering against her long emerald gown. Her hair is black and woven into an elegant knot on the top of her head.

"Good morning, Ms. Bea," Mike calls, waving and smiling from my driveway.

Ms. Bea arches a penciled eyebrow. "What's good about it?" she snarls.

"Sun's shining," Mike goes on. He smiles at the sky for emphasis. "Some nice fluffy white clouds . . ."

"Ease up," I hiss at his side. "You're laying it on too thick."

"She loves it," he whispers back. Then to Ms. Bea he shouts, "Your roses look extra nice today!"

Before she can answer, the rest of the neighbors pour out of their homes and shuffle onto their own manicured lawns. Like Ms. Bea, they're well-dressed—actually they are *overdressed* in uncomfortable-looking, old-fashioned clothes. Their skin looks flawless, and they wear frowns that rival Ms. Bea's. Mike waves and smiles at them, but they ignore him, turning their attention toward their roses and their watering cans just as they have been doing morning after morning for the last two weeks, ever since Mike and I started our investigation.

"You're staring. Pretend to stretch," I whisper, dropping into a forward bend and feeling the familiar burn in the backs of my calves. Mike follows my lead, his head close to mine.

"You see anything new?" he asks.

I peer up at the Oldies, our nickname for our neighbors. "It's hard to see from here," I admit, straining my eyes across the street. "Ms. Attwood's nose looks pointier and slightly crooked. Kind of like a cartoon witch's. You see it?"

Mike peers up from his stretch. "Noted," he says. "Check out Dr. Smith. He's swinging that watering can around way easier than he was last week. It's like his shoulder doesn't bother him anymore."

"Noted." I stand upright and stretch out my quads, signaling for Mike to do the same. I hear Billy scratching at the window, whimpering to get out and join us.

Sorry, bud. It's too hot.

Billy stops scratching, as if he somehow understands, his eyes looking even sadder than normal, sweet brown eyes that have lost their sparkle since Dad died last year.

It was Dad who first suspected that something was up with the Oldies.

"They're kind of creepy, don't you think?" he'd ask Mom and me at dinner. *"It's kind of like they never age. They're old, but not old enough, if you know what I mean."*

"Leave those people alone, James," Mom would plead. *"No one likes living across the street from a nosy cop."*

"What about a nosy daughter?" At this he would smile and ruffle my hair. Together we'd laugh and continue to exchange our theories about the Oldies, despite Mom's

disapproval. In the beginning, we'd

explain stuff: Botox, titanium limbs,

wasn't until later that the more supernatur

to creep in: ghosts, fountains of youth, witch

"You two need to lay off the scary movies,

tell us, rolling her eyes.

At this, Dad would wink at me and whisper, *"W*

her."

I think about Mom's comment as Mike and I contin

stare across the street.

"Maybe they're aliens," I say.

Mike shoots me a look. "That's wild."

"What's wild about it?" I press. "You said so yourself:

they're too weird to be human."

"I didn't mean that *literally*. Maybe they're on some kind

of medication. Don't you watch commercials? Prescriptions

have some pretty major side effects."

I shake my head. "No, this isn't from a pill. This is some-

thing bigger."

Mike's always trying to bring science into things. Where

I see ghosts and ghouls, Mike sees medicine and surger-

ies gone wrong. That's why I didn't want to investigate with

him at first.

Actually, I didn't want to investigate at all after Dad

passed. For months it was impossible to laugh, or run, or

speculate. I couldn't think about the Oldies—that was a Dad

pointless without him,

allowed myself to

d that was only

ne one day

od's *limping kind*

e looked hopeful, his

ath the brim of his signature

ce, it was as if a switch flipped in my brain: *u want this*, I realized. *Dad would want us to inves-te.* Just the thought made me feel close to him again, as if he wasn't really gone.

I study Mike now as his shoulders stiffen. "What's up?" I ask.

"I don't see Mr. Brown," he says, narrowing his eyes as he scans our street.

"He's . . . Wait. You're right. *Where* is he?"

"Make a note," Mike says. "We should go, though. They're starting to look at us."

A chill seeps into my limbs despite the early-June heat. I feel the weight of my neighbors' eyes without even looking at them.

Mike lowers the brim of his hat. "Pond or no pond?"

I look down toward the end of the cul-de-sac, at the dark trees leaning over Goodie Pond. "No pond."

Mike smirks. "Chicken."

"Takes one to know one."

"Whatever, Quinn Parker. Just run."

With this, Mike jets off down the street, and I take off after him, resenting him for the head start. When we reach the corner, he spins around and waves wildly to the Oldies.

"Have a great day!" he cries, at which the neighbors just glare and grind their teeth in a way that makes us both shiver.

"Let's go," I urge, and together, we fly.

CHAPTER 2

For once, Mom is actually home when I get back, and she insists on driving me to school.

I gaze out the window at Mike, who waits for me on the corner. We usually walk to school together and exchange theories, splitting up right before we reach Rocky Hill Middle School so that our friends don't spot us together. No one can know what we're up to. Dad could never get other adults to believe him, and he was a cop. I can't imagine what people would say if they found out about our investigation.

"That's OK, I don't mind walking," I say, pulling my backpack off the kitchen table. I want to talk with Mike about the Oldies. I want to do what Mrs. Carey is always begging us to do in science class: *hypothesize.*

Mom grabs her keys and tucks her cell phone into one of the pockets of her blue nursing scrubs. "Don't be silly, Quinn. My shift doesn't start until eight thirty. Plenty of time." She tosses a dog treat to Billy, who perks his head up slightly from his worn bed, pushed into the spot where Dad used to keep his running shoes.

I frown at Mom's insistence, say goodbye to Billy, and follow her out the door.

It's even more humid on the now-empty street than it was an hour ago, and I think about what a beast track practice is going to be this afternoon.

As if she read my thoughts, Mom says, "Drink lots of water today. We've had a handful of cases of dehydration at the hospital because the kids just didn't drink enough water. Especially at practices."

"I know," I say before flashing an apologetic look to Mike across the street.

Mom notices and waves to Mike. "Hi, Michael! You want a ride to school?"

I feel my face redden as Mike smiles under his Yankees hat. "Good morning, Mrs. Parker," he says, his voice full of charm. "Thanks a lot for the offer, but I'm going to walk."

"You sure?" Mom asks.

"He's sure," I urge. "Let's go."

"I'm sure," Mike agrees.

"OK," Mom says. "Hey, I haven't seen your mom around in a while. Say hi to her for me."

"Will do, Mrs. Parker." Mike tugs on the end of his baseball hat as if he's some kind of cowboy. "Have a good day." His eyes flicker to mine before I fall into the car.

"Such a nice boy," Mom says, turning the key in the ignition. "I've noticed that you've been running together in the morning. Do you two hang out at school?"

"No," I say quickly, turning my head toward the window.

"Must be nice to have a running partner again, you know, since your dad . . ." She trails off, clearing her throat before continuing. "And poor Billy. His arthritis is flaring. He's not much of a running buddy these days."

"Billy's fine," I say. I reach over and push on the radio, making it loud enough to give my mom the hint that I don't feel like talking. Mike throws a slight wave as we drive past. I touch the glass and mouth the word *Later*.

Just as we're about to turn the corner, I spot the front door opening at the Browns' house. Holding my breath, I'm able to make out the toe of Mr. Brown's white sneaker before Mom juts the car in the opposite direction, off of Goodie Lane and onto Main Street.

My fingers tingle as I text Mike: **Are you watching?**

He writes back immediately: ***I'm on it.***

I sink back into the seat, wishing that I was with him. Mom turns down the radio and continues to rattle on beside me, oblivious.

"And Grandma Jane said she might be stopping by tonight..."

At this I perk up. "Really? Is she cooking for us?"

Mom's eyes widen. "You know your grandma. When has she ever gone anywhere without bringing food?"

My whole body warms. No one can cook like Grandma Jane. No one.

"Are you going to be home for dinner?" I ask.

"I can't. I'm working a twelve-hour shift today, unless I get someone to swap with me." I'm not surprised by her words. She's been working more hours at the hospital since Dad passed. "Sorry, honey," she says, turning to face me after she parks in front of the school.

"It's fine," I mumble.

"How about tomorrow you and I go out to dinner? We can go to Cucina Della Nonna if you want. Your favorite."

"Sure," I say, climbing out of the car.

On the sidewalk, I join the sea of seventh graders as we all make our way toward Rocky Hill Middle School. Once inside, I immediately spot Zoe at her locker, and she waves me down in a panic.

"Thank goodness you're here!" she cries, her green eyes widened in relief. "I forgot to do my math homework last night. Can I copy yours? Mrs. Pugliese said she's going to call home if I miss another assignment, and Dad said he will take away my phone if he gets another call . . ."

I dig in my backpack for my math notebook, handing it to Zoe. "Want to come over for dinner tonight?" I ask, swapping the books in my backpack and my locker. "Mom said Grandma Jane might stop by."

"Is she cooking?"

"Yup."

"Then I'm definitely in. I'll meet you after practice."

We chat until the bell rings. I catch a glimpse of Mike just as my homeroom teacher, Mr. Feagin, shuts the door, and I sigh because now I'm not going to get to talk to him until practice. Maybe then we can sneak in a minute or two for him to fill me in about Mr. Brown. But first I have to get through school.

Rocky Hill is painful this time of year. Summer vacation is just a month away, and even the teachers are antsy and twitching.

"I can't *wait* for vacation," Zoe moans at lunch. "I really thought I was going to faint in Language Arts. It reeked." She dissects her sandwich before putting it back together and taking a bite, chewing with her mouth open. Her sparkle lip gloss leaves traces of pink shimmer along the bread.

"Yeah," I agree, cringing. "What *was* that smell?"

Our friend Kaylee looks thoughtful across the table. "It kind of reminded me of feet and pastrami, and some kind of moldy cheese."

Lex puts down her sandwich. "*Hello.* I'm eating."

I take a bite out of my own sandwich: cheddar cheese and pickle slices, my favorite combination. Dad used to make this for me when I was little. I make my own sandwiches now, since Mom doesn't really have time, but even though they're the same ingredients, they don't taste quite as good as when Dad made them.

"Let's just talk about something else," Lex says. "Like my pool! We finally opened it this weekend. I plan on spending the entire summer just floating around and tanning."

"Tanning's so bad for you," Kaylee says matter-of-factly.

"Not with sunscreen."

"Still . . ."

"Whatever, Kay. You know you'll be at my house every day asking to go for a swim."

"Nope. I'll be *running.*" Kaylee looks over at me. "You too, right, Quinn?"

"Definitely running. I need to cut my times before tryouts next year."

Kaylee high-fives me across the table. "Yes! We can train together."

Lex and Zoe exchange looks. "You two are the worst summer vacationers *ever.*"

I toss a slice of soggy pickle at Lex, and she squeals and flicks it on the floor. We both burst out laughing.

Suddenly, Zoe throws herself across the table toward me, her colorful stacked bracelets clicking and chiming against each other. "Mike's staring at you again. I *told* you he's in love with you." Zoe makes eyes in the direction of the boys' table to the right of us. Kaylee, Lex, and I huddle in, settle back, and attempt to discreetly follow her gaze.

"She's right," Lex whispers, giggling. "He's looking right at you."

I drop my sandwich and tug on my ponytail. My neck and my cheeks are hot. This entire cafeteria has gotten too loud. "Stop, you guys," I mutter. "He's not looking at me. We're not even friends."

"That doesn't mean he can't like you," Zoe says.

"He *doesn't*."

Lex smirks. "Then why does he stare at you every day at lunch?"

I chance a peek over: Mike *is* looking at me, but not in any kind of lovey-dovey way. It's more like a *We share a secret* kind of gaze. But seriously, he doesn't have to make it so obvious. I'll have to yell at him later. We can't let people know what we're up to. They'd never in a billion years understand, and their interference could throw off the whole investigation.

Luckily Mrs. Hurd approaches Mike's table, saving us

both from the stares and the giggles. "Mr. Warren," she booms, "it's hot enough in the building today, don't you think? Please remove your hat."

"But Mrs. Hurd—"

"*Hat.*"

We all jump when the lunch bell rings, and I catch Mike let out a sigh of relief as he escapes Mrs. Hurd's clutches.

"Quinn, wait for me by the bike racks after practice," Zoe says. "I'm staying after school for art, so we can skate home together when you're done. I have your board in my locker from when you let me borrow it the other day."

"OK, cool. See you later."

We break off in different directions for our lockers. As I turn, I accidentally slam face-first into Mike. "Ow! Watch where you're going," I cry, feeling myself redden.

He laughs. "You walked into me."

"Why are you following me?" I hiss. "You're making it too obvious. We can't be seen together, remember?"

"Relax, Parker. No one knows what we're talking about. And if anyone asks, we can just tell them I was asking you something about track practice."

I glance nervously from side to side, relaxing only after confirming that my friends are nowhere in sight. "OK, what's up?"

Mike props himself against my locker, his face close to mine. "I saw Mr. Brown."

I lean in closer. "And?"

"He was running sprints up and down the street. Seriously, he's fast. It's like he just appeared out of nowhere."

"But how can that be possible?" I ask. "Yesterday he was limping. He could barely hobble down the front steps to his garden." As I speak, I picture Mr. Brown and his pale, bony legs covered with age spots, legs so skinny that it looks as though you could snap them in two without much effort.

"Define *sprinting*," I tell him.

Mike frowns at me. "Sprinting, sprinting. Like what you and I do after school. Parker, I'm telling you, he was *fast*."

"But *how*?" I press, louder than I intend. I feel the weight of other students starting to stare, and instantly I shrink back against the lockers. Mike holds a finger to his lips as if to shush me.

"We'll talk later. Let's walk home together after practice."

I shake my head. "Can't. Zoe's coming home with me."

"Fine. Tomorrow morning then. Six thirty." He flashes a cheeky smile. "I promise I won't be late this time."

Before I can answer, the second bell rings. Mike gives a last wave and takes off down the hall, ignoring the threats for detention being thrown after him by Mrs. Pugliese.

I don't see him again until after school down at the track. Practice is cut short because of the heat. Coach has us focus on strength and endurance drills instead of running, and he separates the girls from the boys on opposite sides of the field, so there's no time to even try to talk to Mike.

After practice, I grab my backpack from my locker and meet Zoe by the bike racks as planned. She's covered in sparkly gold paint right down to her mismatched Converse. Her dark blond hair is disheveled, her face exhausted, and she's holding her board and mine, as promised.

"What happened to you?" I cry.

"I had a little fight with the paint, but I think I won. I'm going to get an A in that class if it kills me." With that, she hands me my skateboard and we begin the skate home. "How was practice?"

"Same old. I just want to fall on the couch."

"I'm in! Will your mom be home?"

"I don't think so. She said she was working a twelve-hour."

"Does she have ice cream?"

I make a face. "When was the last time *my* mom had ice cream in the house? She barely remembers to buy me the right cereal."

"You should sleep over this weekend. I'll make my dad cook us pancakes. With sprinkles or chocolate chips or something."

"Maybe," I tell her. Dad used to make me pancakes with sprinkles. When I was little, he called them Fancy Cakes. If

Mom had to work a weekend shift at the hospital, he'd make them for me in the morning and then he'd take me over to drop the extras off to Mom.

"Check it out, she's here," Zoe says, nodding to Mom's car in the driveway.

I shrug, and together we make our way inside.

"Hi, girls," Mom greets us from the kitchen. She's still in her scrubs, and Billy is rubbing his head against her shins.

"You coming or going?" I ask, kicking off my sneakers.

"That's a nice hello." Mom frowns. "I'm staying. Maria took my extra shift so that I could get home for dinner. And Grandma Jane called me. She has a very important bridge game tonight and isn't going to make it over here until tomorrow. So we'll have to reschedule our Cucina Della Nonna plans."

"That's fine."

She stretches, her eyes tired and dark. "Do you want to shower first or should I?"

I ruffle Billy's fur. "I will." I always feel disgusting after summer practices and I hate sitting in my own sweat. I run upstairs and shower quickly.

By the time I trot back down, Zoe and Mom have the TV tuned to our favorite dance competition show, with a salad and reheated Chinese takeout spread out like a mini-buffet on the coffee table. Mom's a terrible cook, but she at least *used* to attempt organized meals when Dad was alive: soggy lasagna, overcooked steak—it didn't matter. I used to love dinnertime in our house. Dad would come home all amped up from work, telling us stories about his day and his theories about the Oldies. Now dinner usually consists of Mom, Billy, and me, and a couple of sandwiches between us on the couch.

"How was your day, honey?" Mom asks.

"Fine," I say, collapsing beside her against a pile of throw pillows. Billy quietly spreads out by my feet. "Got an A on my math quiz."

"That's great. Thank goodness you inherited your dad's math skills and not mine. I was always terrible."

Zoe makes a face. "But don't you have to be kind of good at math to become a nurse, Mrs. P?"

"Yup." Mom points her fork at Zoe. "So I had to work my *butt* off."

I spear an egg roll and shove half of the greasy cylinder into my mouth, barely chewing. When Mom's not looking, I sneak a piece to Billy, who swallows it in one grateful gulp. Zoe talks excitedly about which dancers she thinks will go through to the next round. Mom says she likes the dancer that "does the twirly flips." She always uses words like *twirly* when she's tired. She gets predictable. On nights like this, I can bet she'll ask me a few more questions about my day, excuse herself to shower, and fall asleep on the couch while I finish watching my show.

"Did you do your homework?" she asks on cue.

"I'll do it after this."

"Do you have any school forms for me to sign?"

"No."

"How was practice?"

"Hot."

"Did you drink a lot of water?"

"Yup." I hold up my Nalgene bottle for emphasis, taking a big, dramatic swig.

Mom stands up. "I'm going to go shower. You girls clean up during the commercials."

Zoe and I sit cross-legged on the couch with pillows clutched against our chests. Together we laugh and yell at the screen, popping bits of lettuce and fried rice into our mouths, watching as Billy slurps up our litter. Hanging out with Zoe feels like the most natural thing in the world. She was my rock after Dad died, squeezing my hand as I cried myself to sleep every single night for a week, squishing herself into my tiny twin bed and abandoning her own spacious bedroom on the other side of town. When she finally went back home, she called me every night for months, making sure that I was OK.

"I should be a dancer," she muses as the episode finishes and her favorite dancer is eliminated.

"Don't you have to be graceful to dance?"

She throws a pillow at me. "I can be graceful."

I laugh. Zoe is the type of girl who can't peel a banana for lunch without it somehow managing to wind up under her feet. She jumps up to switch off the TV, and then attempts a few twirls in the air before giving up, standing frozen in the middle of the living room. We both watch the black screen for a moment.

"You still thinking about becoming a dancer?"

"Nope. I'm thinking about how my mom's going to be here any minute to pick me up."

"Should we wait outside?"

Zoe groans, dramatically draping her body over the couch. "I guess. It's probably not as hot out anymore."

We throw our dishes in the dishwasher and yell up to my mom before grabbing a juice box to share outside. Billy follows us to the door, and I hook him to his leash. "Told you I'd take you out next time," I whisper. He seems to smile as we make our way out onto the front steps.

Zoe was wrong: It *hasn't* cooled off.

"We *so* shouldn't have to go to school tomorrow," she moans. "There should be laws against making us go to school in this kind of heat."

I notice that Zoe is hogging all of the juice and I yell at her to share. She laughs and squeezes some at me. We're the only noise on the street. There is no sign of life in any of the other houses. It's kind of eerie even though it's not completely dark yet, but then again, Goodie Lane has always felt a bit eerie.

I flash a curious look over to the Oldies' houses, which sit quietly in a row across the street. I remember Ms. Bea earlier this morning, watering her roses, looking as plastic as a mall mannequin, and then I think of Mike and what he said about Mr. Brown. *Parker, he was fast . . .*

"How long do you think the Oldies have lived here?" I ask.

Zoe takes a seat on the top step, motioning for me to join her. "*Forever,*" she says. "Remember when you first moved, and we used to pretend to be detectives? We'd spy on them through your living room window and follow them around the neighborhood. I think we called ourselves the Q and Z Investigators."

"Right! How could I forget? You'd blow our cover every time by laughing whenever we got close."

"Remember that one time with Ms. Bea and Ms. Attwood? They were on some kind of power walk around the pond. We were following them. Ms. Bea heard me giggle and turned around and yelled '*Boo!*'"

I nod. "We ran all the way home."

"Yup. And then we officially closed down the detective business."

I smile at the memory. A pang of guilt punches me in

the stomach as I think about Mike's and my secret, about our own investigation. Part of me wants to tell Zoe about it, but I promised Mike that we'd work alone. Not to mention, it's one thing to be a kid detective when you're seven, but quite another when you're thirteen. But what if . . .

I meet Zoe's eyes. "Seriously, though," I start, "do you think something's up with them?"

Zoe raises an eyebrow. "You want to reopen the case? Get the Q and Z team back in business?" She snorts at the thought before breaking into a full-on laugh that rings out through the now-dark street.

My heart sinks. Her laugh is the only answer I need. I can't tell her about the investigation. Not now. Not ever.

"You still thinking about the neighbors?" she asks.

"No," I lie.

She looks from side to side. "Speaking of which, where is everybody? Your street is so quiet. I feel like we should be whispering."

"I don't know. It's always like this at night."

"You think Mike's home?" she asks.

"How should I know?"

"I never see his parents' cars anymore when I'm here."

I shrug. "I don't see them much either. Mike told me that his dad got promoted. Now he's like the president of the whole university. And his mom works there, too."

Zoe whistles. "Fancy."

"Yup. Mike said it's an extra big deal because his dad is the first African American to run the college."

"That's cool," Ava says. She then flashes me a mischievous smile. "Did he talk to you at practice?"

"Nope, Coach separated the boys and girls today."

"I bet he missed you."

Before I can argue, a pair of headlights flash around the corner of Goodie Lane, and then Zoe's mom eases her car into our driveway.

"Hi, girls," she calls with a smile. "Zoe, you ready?"

"I guess," Zoe mumbles, pulling herself to her feet along with her backpack and her skateboard. "See you tomorrow, Quinn." She hops into the passenger's seat of the car, waving wildly from the window as her mom drives them away.

I remain on the front steps as I watch the headlights fade, leaving Goodie Lane dim and still once again. Billy moans against my leg, signaling for me to take him back inside where it's cool, and lit, and safe.

"Boo!"

I scream as a dark figure pops up from behind the bush to my left, which causes Billy to let out a loud, sharp bark. The monster laughs as he steps into the light.

"Mike!" I cry, barreling forward, ready to throttle him.

Mike's laughing so hard that he's tearing up. "You should have seen your face!"

"Sic 'em, Billy!"

But Billy brightens at the sight of Mike, his tail wagging as he knocks our neighbor to the ground and licks his cheek. The sight of the two of them wrestling around on the grass causes me to smile in spite of my annoyance.

"OK, OK," I say, coaxing Billy back over to me. "Let's go, bud."

Mike scrambles to his feet, pulling his hat back over his eyes. "Wait, weren't you just going to walk Billy?"

"Not anymore," I mutter, trotting down the stairs to take back Billy's leash.

"Aww, don't be like that," Mike says. "I'm sorry. Come on, I'll walk with you." He holds tight to Billy's leash without waiting for an answer and grabs my forgotten juice box with his other hand.

"Hey, that's mine."

Mike smiles as he takes a long sip from the straw. "My mom told me I need more vitamin C in my life."

"She probably meant an orange or a grapefruit, not a juice box."

Mike shrugs and hands it back to me. But of course, it's empty. He laughs. "Relax, Parker. I'll buy you another juice box."

"Let's just walk."

"Fine with me." He takes a beat and then asks, "So what's your latest theory about Mr. Brown?"

I take a thoughtful breath, suddenly remembering a movie Dad and I had watched together. The main character had plastic-looking skin, just like our neighbors, and he was immortal. "Vampire?" I suggest. "Vampires never age, right? Just like the Oldies."

"You know that's impossible, Parker. Besides, the Oldies are always out during the day."

I shrug. "Day vampires."

"What the heck is a day vampire?"

"Simple: a vampire who can come out in the sun."

Mike laughs. "That's not even a thing."

"Yeah it is. Google it."

"No, I'm telling you, Parker: it's something medical, like a procedure or something that's keeping them together."

"*Day vampires.* You'll see."

We've made it to the end of the short street, past the colorful array of old houses belonging to Ms. Bea, Mr. and Mrs. Brown, Ms. Attwood, Dr. and Mrs. Smith, and Mr. Marshall. We stroll all the way to the edge of the cul-de-sac, and before I think to redirect us, we end up at the pond. Both of us stop short at the curb, Billy tugging us backward, away from the dark water.

"It looks kind of creepy tonight, doesn't it?" I breathe.

"It always looks creepy."

We usually don't walk this way at night. Goodie Pond is kind of infamous around here, ever since Mary Hove drowned, way back in the sixties. Rumor has it that her ghost still haunts the waters. It's probably just some stupid urban legend, but our feet still stop short, afraid to go any closer. Billy lets out a low growl just as I see a ripple skate across the surface.

"Do you see that?" I ask, pointing to the water. A mist forms where the ripple ended, rising up in that one spot, almost like a smoke signal. I take a step closer as Mike laughs.

"It's just a frog, Parker," he says, his know-it-all voice cutting through the darkness. "There's like a million in this pond." And then in a flash, his expression morphs into something more sinister, and he holds his hands out in front of him like claws. "Or maybe it's a *ghost*," he teases.

I push him away and scowl. "Don't be so annoying."

"Can't help it. My mom says I have a gift."

I turn back toward the water. For a moment I just watch it, holding my breath, as if daring the mist to rise again.

"Do you really think Mary Hove died in there?" I ask.

"No. It's all fake."

"If it's so fake, then why don't you go touch the surface?"

Mike stiffens. "I've touched it plenty of times."

"So do it again."

"You go touch it."

"Uh-uh, not me. I admit I'm scared! You're the one who doesn't believe in ghosts."

"I'm not afraid of anything." At this, Mike pounds on his chest with his fists.

We both laugh.

"I knew you wouldn't do it," I tell him. "Not as tough as you think, huh?"

"Oh come on, Parker. You're always trying to prove me wrong."

"Because you make it so easy!"

He makes a face. "We'll see about that when I prove you wrong about the Oldies."

The mention of their name makes me shiver. "Let's just go," I say, taking Billy's leash. "My legs feel like they're going to fall off."

We drag ourselves back the way we came. At the edge of the cul-de-sac, Mike pretends to dribble an imaginary basketball and toss it into an invisible hoop, but he trips over his own two feet and nearly stumbles to the ground.

"Wow," I tell him. "Guess you should stick with track."

To my surprise, Mike actually laughs at my joke. We've hit that point in the day when you feel so tired that every little thing becomes silly. We continue walking and giggling, drunk on our own exhaustion and the humidity.

But all of a sudden, Billy stops, cementing his feet to the ground. He lets out another deep growl.

"What's wrong, bud?"

Something about the street looks different. At first, I can't put my finger on what, but then it hits me: all of the Oldies' houses have their front-room lights on. One light per house, and one face per room.

"Are they *watching us*?"

I nod. "Yup."

Sure enough, each neighbor's gaze follows us through their windows, their eyes hollow like skeletons', their mouths twisted and open like they're screaming. I force myself to wave even though my arm feels heavy. Mike follows my lead and waves, too, even though he looks just as stiff as I feel. Not one neighbor waves back.

"Do you think they see us?" I whisper.

"I don't know. Maybe not."

We wave again, this time in more exaggerated motions, but the neighbors don't return the gesture. They continue to stare at us with their gaping mouths. Billy starts to bark—and Billy never barks. I shiver as Mike and I exchange looks. We quicken our pace, not looking back until we reach my front steps.

"Go in," Mike tells me. "I'll wait."

"I'm fine," I hiss back. "Just make sure you lock your door. Go!"

With this I run inside, slamming the door behind me and Billy. With shaking hands I turn the lock, not once but twice, just to be sure.

"Honey, is that you?" Mom calls to me from the couch. "Did I fall asleep again?"

I take a beat and then answer, "Yeah, it's me."

Billy seems to stand guard at the door, quiet now, but alert. Cautiously I peer out the window, checking to make sure that Mike has made it across the driveway to his own house. With relief I see that the street is empty, and the lights from the Oldies' houses have once again been shut off. Peeling myself away from the glass, I finally remember to breathe.

CHAPTER 3

I almost don't go outside the next morning. But I swallow my courage with a Gatorade before hooking Billy to his leash. Billy, for his part, looks wary as he follows me down the front steps. He lets out a low growl from the back of his throat as we both look across the street, searching for signs of life.

And then somebody grabs me around the shoulders. My heart jumps as I spin around, a small scream escaping my lips. Mike bursts into laughter, clutching his stomach as he bowls over.

"Ha! Got you *again*, Parker! You make it *so* easy!"

I clench my fists at my sides, restraining myself from punching him. "What's wrong with you? That was so not funny!"

"It was pretty funny from where I'm standing. *Two* times in a row. That's what I'm talking about!" He continues to laugh, his voice ringing out over the otherwise quiet street. "Oh, I'm sorry, bud," he says, bending over to pet Billy, who looks like he is ready to keel over from fright.

I scowl and turn around so that my back is to Mike as I jog in place, huffing and puffing, my face already hot.

Mike nudges me with his foot. "Don't act like you aren't happy to see me. I even came out early. It's only six twenty."

I nudge him back. "Maybe we should go on separate runs today. We can split up to spy on the Oldies."

"Split up?" He makes a face. "What's the matter? You scared I'll outrun you?"

"Not on your life."

Mike lowers his hat. "Just try and keep up."

I take off before he's ready, Billy's old, graceful legs galloping at my side. I guess that's technically cheating, but it doesn't take Mike long to catch up.

"So that's how it's going to be?" he asks. I ignore him. He passes me and starts running backward. "It's no use fighting it: you'll never run as fast as me."

When he turns back around, I snatch his stupid hat and wave it triumphantly in the air. "I'm sorry, what did you say? *Who's* faster?"

"Hey! Give that back!"

I start running in half circles, back and forth around Goodie Lane, taunting Mike with his hat. "It's mine now!" I cry. I guess I'm louder than I mean to be, because someone behind me clears their throat. I spin around and see Ms. Bea on her front porch, clutching her watering can. Instantly, I shrink back under the weight of her sneer.

"It's early, you realize," she huffs.

"Sorry, Ms. Bea," I say, lowering my voice while still holding firmly to Mike's hat. I notice that once again Ms. Bea is in full makeup, her skin resembling the texture on the plastic watering can.

Mike slows down. "Whatever, wear it. It's not like it's my favorite one." Mike's collection of hats can only be rivaled by Grandma Jane's collection of crystals.

"I think I will," I tell him. The hat's too big, but I like wearing it all the same. I imagine what Zoe would say if she could see me right now, frolicking in the street with Mike Warren.

"So," Mike starts, bobbing up and down beside me. "Last night was weird, right?"

"They're ghosts," I say. "I was thinking about it. It's the only logical explanation."

"There's nothing *logical* about ghosts, Parker. They don't exist. Just like vampires don't exist, just like aliens don't exist . . ."

I turn to him, my skin suddenly hot. "Then how do *you* explain last night?"

He shrugs. "Optical illusion."

"What?"

"You know, optical illusion. It's what happens when the brain processes reflected light and—"

"OK, OK." I wave him off before he gets too technical. "I forgot you're all like Bill Nye the Science Guy over here."

"You can't argue with facts, Parker."

"You don't have *facts*, Mike. You have *theories*."

Mike pouts and we both turn our attention back across the street. More of the Oldies have made their way outside— all of them except Mr. Brown.

Mike notices, too. "Yesterday Mr. Brown didn't come out until later," he says in a low voice. "Maybe if we want to spot him, we should go on the run first and try to catch him after—maybe as we cool down in your driveway."

"Sounds like a plan," I agree.

Together we wave goodbye to a scowling Ms. Bea as we start running in the direction of the pond toward the trail. I can feel myself climbing into that peaceful state of mind where I don't think of anything else except my breath, the ground, my body—I'm focused until we reach the water. Then, from the corner of my eye, I catch a glimmer of orange light breaking through the surface. *What is that?* I continue to squint as we jog closer to the edge. *Is that a fish?* I slow my pace just as the color fades.

"Come on," Mike urges, pulling my attention away from the water. "It's too muddy over here. Let's head on back to Goodie. We can run sprints instead."

With this, I follow him for one last loop before heading back toward Goodie Lane.

We're just about to launch into our sprint exercises when, all of a sudden, there are footsteps behind us. Loud and fast. *Thump-thump-thump-thumpthumpthump.* They grow closer and more aggressive.

"Parker, look out!" Mike pulls me out of the way just in time.

Next thing I know, I'm in Mike's arms, staring at the backside of skinny, eighty-something-year-old Mr. Brown. He turns around and shouts at us, "Share the road!" before taking off in another sprint. Billy is barking his head off and Mike grabs his leash to keep him from darting after Mr. Brown.

"You OK?" Mike asks.

I don't answer. I stare down the street after our neighbor. Two days ago I watched him struggle to limp his way out of his house.

"That's wild," Mike mumbles, catching his breath, petting Billy's head to soothe him. "It's like he got new legs or something."

"Maybe he did," I say, half joking, as I point to the thick bandage wrapped around his right calf.

Mike follows my gaze. "Remember when Ms. Bea had her whole face bandaged a week ago?"

I do. Last week, on Monday, she came out of her house as usual at six thirty, dressed in her evening gown and armed with a watering can. Only, instead of her face being painted, it was bandaged with thick white gauze, wrapped around and around as though she were a mummy. A mummy wearing designer heels and a topknot.

But the next day, the bandages were gone and her face once again looked perfect. *Too perfect.*

"You think they both had surgery or something?" Mike asks.

I shrug, my attention focused on Mr. Brown. Just before he disappears toward the pond, his bandage gets caught by a stray bush branch, exposing the skin beneath.

And now I see it: the scar. Back of the right leg, middle calf, shaped like Florida, about the size of a glue stick.

"Whoa, Parker, where you going on me?"

I'm on the ground, dizzy and light-headed. "That's—"

"I think you need some water." Mike looks nervous. He gently removes his hat from my head and brushes back my bangs. "Are you too hot?"

I shrug.

He offers a weak smile and jokes, "Running with me will do that to you."

"I'm fine. I think I just need to eat breakfast," I lie, as Mike helps me stand up.

In truth, I'm thinking about my dad. My dad was a fast runner, a sprinter in college. He was always ahead of me as we ran together in the mornings, so I had plenty of opportunities to stare at the backs of his legs, to stare at his scar.

He got it on the job. A dog bit him, and it took twelve stitches to sew his calf back together. It was such an unusually shaped scar. Shaped like Florida. Seeing an identical one on someone else takes my breath away.

Mike is watching me intently. "What happened? Was it Mr. Brown?"

I shake my head. "No, I just need to eat something. I'm fine. I can walk." I step back from his grip, proving that I'm able to move on my own. He remains at my side until we reach my front porch. I look out across the street toward our neighbors' houses, half expecting to see them watching me again. I think of last night with their skeletal faces in the windows and try to shake away the heavy feeling in my stomach.

"Thanks for the run," I mutter to Mike, taking Billy's leash back.

"Are you sure you're OK?"

"I'm *fine*. Go home, Mike."

"Are we walking to school together?"

"Sure. I'll meet you on the corner."

"Cool." With this, Mike lowers his hat back onto his head and saunters off.

When he's gone, I close the door, unhook Billy, and escape up to my room, my legs still feeling weak. I immediately start riffling through old family photos from my shoebox collection, separating them into hurried, haphazard piles on my bed. It doesn't take long before I find the one I'm looking for—it's a shot of Dad at the beach wearing his favorite shark-printed swim trunks, looking out into the waves. Most important, when I took the picture I captured his whole body, including the backs of his legs, including his scar shaped like Florida.

I tuck my dad's picture into my backpack before hastily putting the rest of the photos away. I get myself ready for school in a daze, convincing myself that I didn't see what I thought I saw. When seven thirty hits, I say goodbye to Billy, grab an apple and my backpack, and head out the door. Mike is already waiting for me outside.

I smooth down my hair, wishing I had spent just a little longer in front of the mirror.

"You look better," Mike says, studying my face. "You should really eat that apple though so you don't faint again."

"I didn't faint."

"You almost did," Mike says. "Face it, Parker. I basically

saved your life." He flashes me that cocky smile of his as I look out across the street.

The Oldies are all out and about, gardening, sipping mugs of tea, reading the paper on their front porches. Mike nudges me and points over to Mr. Brown, who is stretching out his calves by his front steps. His wife is sweeping the sidewalk.

"Nice run, Mr. Brown," Mike calls over. I want to smack him in the arm, but instead I play it cool and take a large bite of my apple to keep myself from talking.

It's as if all of the Oldies suddenly stop what they're doing at once, like figurines in a music box that just ran out of song.

Mr. Brown smiles hard in our direction. "Not bad, right? I could have given Quinn's old man a run for his money."

I freeze, mid-bite. Mr. Brown continues to smile.

"No offense, but you couldn't hold a candle to Mr. Parker," Mike says. He's no longer smiling, and he takes what feels like a protective step in front of me. I become aware of my heart beating faster.

"Don't you have somewhere to be, dears?" Ms. Bea is now edging toward us with graceful steps, her heels leaving indentations in the damp grass. She's also smiling, with her red painted lips, but her eyes remain serpent-like as they narrow in on me and Mike. Her cheekbones jut out to make her look almost skeletal, and once again I'm reminded of last night and the hollow faces in the windows.

Suddenly, beads of icy water hit the front of my arms and legs. Ms. Bea screams.

"Whoa, sorry, Bea," Mr. Marshall calls from his front yard. He's wrestling with a garden hose, spraying all of us in the process. Ms. Bea gets hit the worst, and her lavender silk dress turns a deep shade of plum.

"*You! Fool!*" she cries.

"Sorry!" Mr. Marshall calls. "Faulty valve." He looks at Mike and me as we shake off the excess water from our backpacks. "You all right, kids?" I notice that his tone is softer than the other Oldies', even when they're trying to act nice. His eyes also seem warmer. Kinder. It makes me stiffen. I don't trust it.

"We're good," Mike says, waving him off. "Let's go, Parker. I think that's our cue to leave."

Mike leads me over to the sidewalk as the other Oldies rush to check on Ms. Bea, who's trudging back across the grass, pulling up the front of the sopping dress in her hands. Mr. Brown bends over to carry Bea's train, and I can't help but peek at his leg before Mike and I turn the corner. The bandage is back in place.

"What a bunch of weirdos," Mike mutters.

"Yeah, something about them is *definitely* weird." I exchange looks with Mike. "And it's our job to figure out what."

CHAPTER 4

My head is still fuzzy at school. I see Mike in the hallway before first period and he asks me how I'm feeling. I tell him I'm fine and try not to notice the way his lips slightly pucker when he's concerned.

Zoe notices me notice. "What was *that* all about?"

"Nothing," I say quickly. "Come on, we're going to be late."

"Late shmate," she says. Her eyes widen. "Did something happen? Is there like a *thing* between you two?"

"There's no *thing*." I start walking faster.

But Zoe's not letting me off that easy, even as we enter our classroom and take our seats in the corner. "Sorry," she says, "but that was most definitely a thing."

"We were just talking about something from track," I lie, not meeting her eyes. "You know, from practice." I clear my throat and fidget in my chair. "It's fine, though. It's nothing."

Zoe studies me for a moment before shrugging. "Whatever," she says. I can't tell whether or not she believes me, but I'm relieved that she at least lets the subject drop.

The bell rings, and Ms. Pennell starts her lesson for the day. We're talking about some Langston Hughes poem, but I can't tell you which one because my mind is a mile away, back on Goodie Lane. I wonder what Mr. Brown is doing right now. Did he go to work today?

He and his wife are the owners and directors of Phoenix Funeral Home. It's the only funeral home in town. Supposedly it's been in the Brown family for generations, and like the Browns themselves, the Phoenix is a local icon. Mom used it for Dad's memorial service, despite Grandma Jane begging her to look elsewhere. Mom said she didn't have it in her to "shop around," so Dad's wake was held at the Phoenix.

The Phoenix seemed like a typical funeral home. There were different rooms to choose from, yet they all looked the same with their muted colors and potted plants. Mom liked Mrs. Brown, but I always thought both of the Browns were mean.

Mrs. Brown in particular doesn't talk much, but when

she does it's usually something judgmental like "Get a haircut!" She's best friends with Ms. Bea—in fact, all of the Oldies are pretty tight. Unless they're at work or just stepping out quickly, they usually travel in packs, and despite being liked enough by people around town, they never have visitors. Well, except Grandma Jane that one time . . . I make a mental note to ask her for details the next time I see her—maybe tonight at dinner.

I wonder if Grandma Jane has any of her own ideas about the Oldies. Whenever Dad and I used to talk about it, she didn't chime in.

My mind runs through all of the theories I've spent hours researching online, from ghosts, to aliens, to day vampires.

But on the other hand, what if Mike's right? What if there's a simple explanation for all of this?

Maybe I was just really tired this morning and my eyes didn't see what they thought they saw. Maybe Mr. Brown wasn't really going that fast, maybe it just *seemed* that way because Mike and I were so busy fooling around and not going our usual speed. Maybe I got the scar wrong. Maybe there was no scar.

Or maybe it's all real.

Mike's theory about the Oldies' surgeries can't explain how Mr. Brown is suddenly able to sprint, when just last week he could barely walk. It also doesn't explain why he now has legs identical to my father's. And what about

Ms. Bea and her ageless face—bandaged one day, fresh the next?

I bet if I sat here long enough, I could think of strange things about all the other Oldies, like how Ms. Attwood seems taller than a month ago, and how Dr. Smith is able to move large boxes every Saturday from his car to his garage. And why doesn't anyone seem to know how old they all are? How did they all come to live on the same street?

I start to bounce in my chair: I want to talk to Mike, to recap what we saw this morning, but the only class we have together is science. Today, Mrs. Carey shows us a documentary about the human body, so we aren't able to properly speak until after school at track practice.

"I have to talk to you," I whisper on the field. I make pointed eyes toward my shoelace, and as I bend down to retie it, Mike takes a large step away from his circle of friends, before bending down and pretending to tie his own shoe.

"What's up, Parker?"

"Are we being ridiculous?" I whisper.

"You might be. I know I'm not."

"Seriously," I urge. "Did we really see what we thought we saw? Was Mr. Brown really sprinting?"

Mike's face turns serious. "He was most definitely sprinting. Come on, Parker. You know something is up. We just have to find out what. My money's still on some type of experimental old people's surgery . . ."

Before I can reply, Coach barks at us: "Parker! Warren! Get back to your teams. It doesn't take *that* long to tie a shoe, for crying out loud."

We both jump up at the same time, bonking our heads together in the process.

"Ow!"

"Ugh!"

"You need to look out—"

"That was *your* fault—"

"Parker! Warren! Quit clowning around and get moving!" Coach hollers.

Mike and I exchange looks before rejoining the action.

Coach immediately pairs Jess and me together. She's the best one on the team. She's the reason I get up early every morning and run before school on drill days. As much as I like her, I still want to beat her, and I know we're both trying out for team captain next year. We're cool and everything, but I wouldn't say we're friends. I think we're too competitive for that.

"Now listen," Coach explains, "I want to time you girls for the one-hundred-yard dash."

Ugh! I hate sprinting, and my legs still feel wobbly from this morning. "But, Coach, I thought it was a drill practice now," I say, my tone much more whiny than I intend.

Coach frowns at me. "What's that, Quinn? Are you saying *you can't*? Is that what I'm hearing?"

"No, Coach. I can." Coach has this rule that anyone who says "I can't" has to drop and do an unspecified number of push-ups right here on the track.

A drop of sweat trickles down my nose. He narrows his bushy eyebrows and nods. "That's what I thought. Now get yourselves ready, I'll give you the signal."

I see Jess stiffen beside me before we march down to take our places.

"Ladies, take your marks."

Jess and I set ourselves up on the starting blocks. I make a conscious effort to control my breathing, to concentrate, to ignore the cheers from our teammates looking on. I pretend I don't hear Mike's voice ring out and call my name.

"Set. Go!"

We dash into a wall of heat—and for about two strides I'm actually *in front* of Jess! *I can do this,* I think. *I can beat her.* And within a blink, I am blinded by my own sweat—I feel it stinging my eyes and choking my throat, and the next thing I see are Jess's calves pounding down in front of me. I'm reminded of Mr. Brown. I'm reminded of my father, of the familiar Florida-shaped scar that I used to stare at each morning that we ran together as I followed behind him down Goodie Lane. *Get it together, Quinn,* I tell myself.

But it's no use—it feels like I'm running on a treadmill, going nowhere. I push, and push, and fall farther and farther behind.

And then it's over. I spin onto the ground. Jess and Coach lean over me.

"You OK, kid?" Coach asks, concerned. His face looks like a black circle, a blind spot from the beaming sun behind him. "Quinn?"

The dizziness sets in. I'm floating. I'm on a boat. I'm on a cruise. I'm anywhere but here.

Someone puts a bottle of water in my hand and instinctively I chug. Mom's words ring in my ears: *We've had a handful of cases of dehydration at the hospital because the kids just didn't drink enough water*. I chug some more while Coach coaxes me to take deep breaths. "I've never seen her like this," I hear him say.

I hear the assistant coach's voice ask if they need to call the nurse. Or an ambulance.

At this I wave my hands. "I'm fine."

"Quinn."

Their faces come back into view. Coach, the assistant coach, Kaylee, and Jess are huddled around me, with all of my teammates looking on from safe distances.

"Is she OK, Coach?" Mike asks, stepping forward.

"She will be," Coach says. "Mike, take her home, but not until you stop at the nurse's office and get the all clear."

Mike nods and pulls me to my feet. "Come on, Parker. Time to go."

Still dizzy, I lean on him for support during the walk up the hill, ignoring the chorus of *oohs* and *ahhs* from our teammates.

"Sorry," I mumble when we reach the building, afraid to meet his eyes.

"Too hot to run anyway," he says. "Let's go see the nurse and get you home."

"This is overkill. I just need some water."

"So drink it in the nurse's office. I'm not about to get yelled at by Coach for not taking you."

"Fine. Whatever." I let him lead me down to Mrs. Rushall's office, where we sit in ice-cold air-conditioning for twenty minutes, drinking water and sharing orange slices while Mrs. Rushall checks my vitals and deems me fit to walk home with Mike, but only after she calls my mom and the two of them have a forever conversation about the importance of hydration.

Eventually, Mike and I make our way home together in silence.

We stop in front of my house, and a wave of relief rushes over me as I spot Grandma Jane's bright blue car in the driveway.

"Something smells good," Mike says, sniffing the air dramatically.

"Yeah." I smile. "My grandma's the best cook."

Mike looks at me. "You going to be OK, Parker?"

"Yeah, I think I just need to cool off in the air-conditioning for a bit."

Before Mike can respond, a familiar voice cuts through the humid air. "Share the road!" *Thumpthumpthump*...

Mike and I spin around just in time to see Mr. Brown sprinting past us at top speed. He's wearing red running shorts that hit just above his knees, exposing a pair of tanned and toned legs that seem too young to be attached to his body. He skids to a halt a few feet away from us, launching into a series of lunges as if they were no big deal.

I squint and stare at the all-too-familiar Florida-shaped scar, which for whatever reason is no longer covered by a bandage. I'm much closer to it now than I was this morning and am able to make out the little curves and edges, along with the series of small brown freckles that form a Little Dipper on the upper left of his calf.

"Brown is *destroying* those lunges," Mike says in awe.

"My dad was always practicing those," I say, feeling dizzy again.

"I remember."

I kind of like that he remembers.

"I can't get over this guy," Mike adds, still looking at Mr. Brown, who begins bouncing from side to side and shaking out his arms like a boxer before a big fight. "You think he got new meds or something? How is he *doing* that?"

Something feels *wrong*. The familiarity seems *wrong*. The scar, the freckles, the quick feet, the slightly out-turned toes, and tan legs. It makes my head hurt. I blink and stare, blink and stare. Finally, I unzip my backpack, digging around until I find the beach photo from this morning. I thrust it in front of Mike. "Look."

Mike laughs and says, "Nice shark bathing suit, Mr. Parker," and then he suddenly stops smiling. His brown eyes widen. He lifts his hat brim off his forehead and takes the picture from my hand. I watch him look from the photo to Mr. Brown, and back again. He gasps, "Is that?"

"Yes."

"But it can't—"

"I know. But look, it *is*."

"There has to be a logical explanation for this," Mike breathes.

I brace myself against the pavement. "There is an explanation," I tell him, taking back the picture. "It just isn't logical."

CHAPTER 5

"There she is!" Grandma Jane cries as I fall through the front door. "My special girl. Come, come, drop that heavy backpack. I made your favorite chicken potpie."

I throw my arms around her despite how sweaty I am, breathing in her familiar scent of lavender and rosemary, courtesy of the homemade oils that she always dabs on her wrinkled skin and runs through her mane of gray hair.

Billy pushes his wet nose against my legs, waiting for his own greeting. "Is Mom home?" I ask as I bend down to scratch his neck.

"Sorry, dear. She got called in, so you'll have to make do with little old me." She smiles at Billy. "Well, me and sweet Billy boy." She pats his head and nods over to the kitchen.

"Come on, honey. Let's eat before it gets cold. I've had it rewarming in the oven."

Just the scent of Grandma Jane's chicken potpie is enough to erase everything else about today. I collapse into my chair and watch Grandma Jane dance around the room, her many bracelets and crystal necklaces clinking as she moves. I notice a candle burning on the counter. Grandma Jane makes those, too, and she dries her own herbs, which she insists on hanging in our kitchen window. For what, I'm not sure, but she never seems to use them for cooking. I think these things used to annoy Mom, but now the house feels warmer when Grandma Jane is here, even just in spirit.

She pulls the pie out of the oven, the crust golden brown, oozing with creamy goodness. My stomach growls as she slices into it and sets down a giant piece in front of me.

"Bon appétit!" she says merrily, joining me across the table.

I take a bite and swoon. "Best. Ever," I tell her.

She laughs, delighted. "Eat up. There's plenty more where that came from." She tosses a piece of the crust to Billy, whose eyes light up in a way that I haven't seen since Dad was alive.

Grandma Jane turns back to me and smiles. "So fill me in. Tell me about school. Track. All the things."

"I have a big meet coming up against Bedford."

"That so? I'll start making my glitter signs, then." Her face turns serious. "Speaking of track, what happened today? Your mother got a call from the coach, so she asked me to come check on you. Something about you fainting?"

I freeze mid-bite. "I didn't faint." I feel the weight of her gaze and add, "I just got dizzy."

"From the heat, or something else?"

"The heat," I lie. "Definitely the heat."

"You're drinking enough water, right?" She narrows her eyes. "Do I have to talk to that coach? Is he not giving you breaks?"

"He gives us breaks," I insist. "I guess I just should have drunk a little bit more."

She reaches across the table and brushes my hair away from my eyes. I feel safe in this moment, like I can trust my grandma with anything.

"Can I ask you something?"

She looks at me. "Anything, dear."

"What happened that day you went to Ms. Bea's house?"

Grandma Jane pulls back slightly, making a face. "Why do you want to talk about *her*?"

I shrug. "I just never really see anyone else going over there. You must have been special."

At this she grins. "Darn right. And don't you forget it."

"So what happened? What was she like? What was her house like?"

Grandma Jane scrunches up her face and fingers the green crystal hanging from her neck. "Her house is taste-less, just like her."

"But what happened?"

"Nothing happened," she says, shrugging. "She's weird, is all."

"Weird how?"

"Oh, you know—obsessed with youth. Obsessed with being young. Kept asking me all of these questions about 'Wouldn't you like to be younger?' and 'Don't you wish your body could have a tune-up?' I could tell right away she just invited me over to sell me something. Probably some of those overpriced creams from her shop. Lord only knows."

I can feel my mouth hanging open, desperate for more. "Did she ever say what she wanted?"

"I didn't stick around long enough to find out," she says. "I tell you, your daddy was right! Something is off about Bea and the rest of those people." She waves her hand in the air, dismissing the rest of the conversation. "Now, I don't want to waste our time talking about those old bores. What do you say we slice another piece and I can tell you about how I wrecked everyone at bridge last week?"

Despite having many more questions, I let them go as Grandma places another slice of pie in front of me. We continue to talk about normal things until the sunlight starts to fade outside.

"Come and give your grandma another squeeze before I go."

I fall into her arms as we say our goodbyes. When she pulls away, she stares deep into my eyes. "You take care of yourself, you hear me? You have to be careful."

Her words echo in my mind, and part of me can't help but wonder if she is only talking about track.

"I'll be careful," I promise.

She hovers with her hand over my cheek, the touch so warm and tender that I melt completely into it.

"Sorry I missed dinner last night," Mom says the next morning, handing me a granola bar. "Grandma Jane really outdid herself on that pie though. Best ever, am I right? I had two helpings."

"Yeah, I love when she cooks for us," I admit, stuffing the granola bar into my backpack. "Are you home tonight?"

"Sorry, honey. I'm picking up a few extra shifts this month."

I don't answer as I tie my shoelaces, but I can feel her watching me.

"How about I drive you to school?" she offers. "We can stop at the bakery and grab a donut on the way if you want."

"No thanks," I say quickly. That was Dad's thing: we'd

go for a run in the morning, spy on the Oldies a bit, and then he'd stop at the bakery and buy me a chocolate glazed donut on the way to school. The thought of going through that ritual without him makes me feel sick.

Mom runs a gentle hand through the end of my ponytail. "How about just the ride, then? We'll forget the donut."

"Sure," I say, before waving goodbye to Billy and heading for the door.

On the way out of the house, Mom realizes she forgot her work badge and has to run back inside to grab it. I wait out by the car, leaning against the passenger's door and stretching my face up toward the sun.

"You should wear sunscreen," a voice calls from across the street. "Keeps you young."

My eyes follow the voice, and I'm surprised to see Ms. Bea standing on her front stoop, looking right at me. She's wearing a solid-red A-line dress paired with heels and a thick gold chain, coiled around her neck like a snake.

"Hi, Ms. Bea," I say meekly.

She cocks her head to one side and smiles stiffly. One exaggerated step at a time, she comes toward me. "I bet you never wear sunscreen," she says. "Do you?"

I bob my head up and down like a ventriloquist's dummy. "Yeah, I do," I tell her, planting my feet more firmly on the pavement. "Just not when I'm going to school."

"Figures. You kids never appreciate your youth." She

spits out the words so that they hover in the air like angry wasps. "You don't *deserve* your youth."

There is a moment when the sun hits her face just right, and there is something terrifying about her illuminated expression.

"Sorry, Quinnie, I'm ready!" Mom calls, locking the front door behind her and jogging down the steps. Her voice cuts through the tense air and brings relief back to my limbs. "Good morning, Ms. Bea."

Ms. Bea retreats onto her lawn and smiles innocently back at my mother, every trace of menace hidden. "Good morning, dear. I was just telling your daughter how beautiful she's gotten." She winks at me and I step closer to the car.

Mom unlocks the doors and tosses her bags on the back seat. "Hasn't she? She looks just like my husband."

"It must break your heart," Ms. Bea says, her voice all honey and charm.

Mom takes a beat before answering, changing the subject. "Your roses are gorgeous again this year. What's your secret? Mine never seem to bloom."

Ms. Bea shrugs one shoulder. "I have a way with nature."

"Lucky you," Mom says. "Well, we've got to run. You take care."

"You too, dear. Goodbye, Quinn. See you soon." She smiles again at me, and I climb into the car without answering.

Mom scolds me as she starts the engine. "That was rude. Ms. Bea said goodbye to you, Quinn."

"So?" I challenge. "She's mean and always has been."

Mom eases the car out of the driveway and onto Goodie Lane. "That's not true. She's perfectly nice."

"Oh, come on, Mom. You have to admit that she's weird. All of the Oldies are."

"What have I told you about calling them that?"

I don't respond. Mom exhales a deep breath before relaxing her grip on the steering wheel. She changes the subject and asks me questions about school and track. I humor her with my automated answers, but her small talk isn't much of a distraction from the million questions fogging up my head.

"Bye," I mumble as we pull up to school. I'm about to hop out when Mom tugs on my sleeve.

"Honey, I . . ." She trails off.

"What?"

It takes her a moment to answer, but when she does there's a sadness to her voice. "Remember that you're on your own for dinner again."

"It's fine. I'll eat Grandma Jane's leftovers."

Mom bites her bottom lip. "I promise I'll get a night off soon. We'll have some time. Just the two of us."

It's always just the two of us, I want to say. But her eyes look so sad that it causes a lump to form in my throat. "OK,

Mom," I tell her. "That sounds good." I gently pull my arm away and open the car door. "See you later."

"Bye, honey."

I keep my head down as I make my way inside the building.

Zoe is already waiting at my locker. "Tell me everything."

I brace myself but play it cool. "What?"

"Some little birdies told me that Mike Warren walked you home after practice."

"So? He lives next door to me. He was really just walking himself home."

"That's not what I heard."

"From who? Kaylee? Lex? *Jess?*"

"I heard that you fainted and he had to carry you up the hill in his big strong arms—"

"Seriously, Zoe! It wasn't even like that! I didn't faint."

"Did he walk you home?"

I close my locker. "Kind of."

"I knew it!" Zoe squeals. She grabs my purse from my arm and begins riffling through it. "Aha!" Before I can stop her, she pulls out my phone.

"Zoe!"

But it's too late. She finds what she's looking for: a message thread from Mike. I'm so amateur. I should have used a passcode or an alias like "Aunt Sally" or something, but no, there it is in black and white. Mike Warren's name in my contact list, alongside two fresh texts that I haven't even gotten to read yet. Zoe has a mini-meltdown on our way to homeroom.

"I mean, a guy likes you and I have to find out about it from someone else? Why didn't you *tell* me? I'm your best friend. Doesn't that count for anything anymore?"

Mike approaches before I can answer, and I can't quite decide if his presence is a blessing or a curse given the conversation. Obliviously, he nods to both of us.

"Sup, Parker. Hey, Zoe." Zoe stares back at him with widened, expectant eyes. Mike turns to me. "Parker, can I talk to you for a second?"

Zoe continues to stare. I'm mortified and really hope that I'm not blushing. "Yeah, sure. I'll see you after lunch, Zoe," I mumble before I take off with Mike down the hall in the opposite direction.

"What's up with her?" he asks.

"Zoe? Nothing, she's fine."

He smiles. "She likes me, doesn't she? I catch her staring at me all the time during lunch."

I burst out laughing.

Mike frowns. "What's so funny?"

"You think—" I can't even finish my sentence because I'm laughing so hard. People are looking at us as they walk by. "You think she likes . . ."

"Oh come on, Parker." He flashes a smile. "Am I *that* bad?"

"Well, now that you mention it."

"Hey!"

"Actually," I tell him, "she thinks that *we're* together." I snort and look at him, ready for him to laugh. Only, he doesn't: he just blinks.

"Did you tell her we were?" he asks.

I can feel the heat trickling around my neck and up my cheeks. "No! Why would I say that?"

He steps in closer. "Because think about it, Parker. It's the perfect cover."

"Cover?"

"Yeah, for why we're together all the time. Instead of trying to deny it, we should just say we're going out."

My throat feels scratchy all of a sudden, but I somehow manage to choke out the words, "Going out? Like *together* going out?"

Now Mike laughs. "What else would I mean?"

The hallway is too crowded: I feel warm all over and I just want to run. But he's right. I mean, he's at least kind of right: lying to our friends would at least get them off our case while we investigate the Oldies.

"OK," I tell him, not meeting his eyes. "Fine, let's do it. But only until we figure out what's going on with our neighbors. I never lie to Zoe."

"It's just a little lie," he says.

"Not really!"

He shrugs and moves to slide an arm around my shoulders. I dodge out of his reach.

"What are you doing?"

"Pretending to be your boyfriend."

"Not *yet*," I tell him. "Let me at least wrap my head around it."

"Whatever you say, Parker. Anyway, listen. I've got to talk to you about something else."

I quiet down as he pulls in closer. We lean against a row of deserted lockers. "What happened this morning?" I whisper. "Did you run?"

"Yeah, by myself, no thanks to you."

"It wasn't my fault," I argue. "Mom wouldn't let me go out because of yesterday."

"Whatever. It doesn't matter. I saw our guy. You were right. Check this out." Mike holds out his cell phone to me and I gasp at a photo of the back of Mr. Brown's leg. The scar!

"He was sprinting again," Mike continues. "So I started racing him. He was too fast."

"But he's *ancient*," I breathe.

"Exactly. But there was this one moment when he stopped running to tighten his laces, so that's when I got the shot. He noticed me standing behind him and asked me what I was doing."

"Oh my gosh, what did you say?"

"I asked him how he got the scar."

I hate my mother for keeping me inside this morning. "And?"

"He looked like he wanted to rip my head off just for asking. But he answered. He said a dog bit him."

I feel a burst of cold rush through me. "You're lying."

"That's what he said, and then he just sprinted off again. I tried to catch him but he was too fast."

The first bell rings and I remain frozen. "Parker," Mike urges. "We got class. Come on, Parker, move."

I remember back to a moment on Goodie Lane. It was a school night after dinner, and Dad was taking the garbage out in a pair of old running shorts. I was helping him drag the bags to the curb. Mr. Brown was also dragging his trash bags to the overflowing bin on the street, only he had tons of them, like five or six. I remember thinking that was a lot of garbage for just two people. Dad started making small talk like he was prone to do whenever we ran into the Oldies. I remember that both of them were limping, which Dad found to be really funny for some reason. Mr. Brown was complaining about arthritis, and Dad was telling him about the dog bite.

I grab Mike's arm and squeeze. "Mr. Brown knows that's what happened to my dad! Don't you understand? That's how my dad got *his* scar."

Mike's eyes widen. "We'll talk after school," he says, and darts down the hallway before the second bell rings.

Zoe naturally questions me about Mike as soon as I get to our shared class. An intricately folded note pops onto my desk when Ms. Pennell's back is turned.

Be honest, the note reads. *Are you dating Mike Warren?*

I stare at the words longer than I need to, before taking the biggest breath and writing *Yes*. I toss the note back to her and watch how large her eyes get. She mouths the words *I knew it!* All I can do is shrug.

Word travels fast. Too fast. Everyone in the school seems to know about my fake relationship by lunch. Zoe and the rest of the girls stare at Mike's crowded table even more than usual, and I don't bother to try to stop them. Mike, for his part, calmly sits and eats his cheeseburger as his many friends laugh around him. When he's done, he throws his trash away before sauntering over to me.

"Sup, Parker." He smiles in a way that makes me blush for real. "Can I sit down for a minute?"

All I can do is nod as Zoe nudges me in the ribs, smiling like an idiot. I guess I can't really blame her; if this romance were real, then I would be the first one of our friends to go out with anybody at Rocky Hill.

But it's not real. It's all pretend. And even though my

shoulders turn to mush when he places his arm around them, this lie is just that: a lie. A means to an end, and by *end*, I mean an end to the Oldies.

The gossip mill follows me for the rest of the day, and I've never been so happy to get to the track. Coach pairs me off with Jess again, and the two of us are stuck running drills against each other.

"You sure you feel OK today?" Coach asks, his bushy eyebrows raised so high that they almost disappear into his hairline. "No fainting, I hope?"

"No, Coach," I mumble. "I'm fine."

And to prove it, I run faster than ever, smashing my old times and beating Jess in the process.

"Who lit a fire under your feet today?" Coach praises, high-fiving me so hard that my palm stings.

I beam. "I don't know, Coach. Must be all that rest I got on the field yesterday."

Coach laughs. "Keep it up, Parker." He blows his whistle and turns to the team, signaling everyone together.

I turn to say something to Jess, but she's moved away from me. Her arms are folded across her chest and she's scowling. Under any normal circumstance, I'd be upset to the point of losing sleep, but given everything going on with the Oldies, I don't have the energy to care.

"Huddle up!" Coach yells, clapping his hands.

The team forms a circle around Coach as we listen to him talk about the importance of light feet, lots of water, and eight hours of sleep. When he blows the final whistle, I make eyes at Mike, who like always is in the center of a circle. He nods at me and says goodbye to his friends before joining me up the hill.

"We need a plan," he states, swinging his backpack over his shoulder and lowering his hat against his forehead.

"Maybe we could start at the library? Or in my dad's filing cabinets."

"Boring."

"Well, what were *you* thinking?"

"Something a bit more dangerous than that. Like sneak into one of their houses or something."

"Whatever, Mike. I'm not even going to talk about this with you if you aren't going to take it seriously."

"I am taking it seriously. Come on, Parker. What other options do we have?"

I don't answer, because he's probably right. "We can't break into Mr. Brown's house. I'm not doing anything illegal."

"OK, OK, well what if we didn't *break* in? What if we were *invited* in?"

I shake my head. "There's no way Mr. Brown is going to invite us in. No one other than other Oldies have ever been inside those houses." I think for a moment before adding, "Well, except for Grandma Jane."

Mike perks up. "Cool! Then let's just ask your grandma to help us."

"That won't work. She and Ms. Bea kind of hate each other. There was this whole thing. Grandma Jane thought Ms. Bea was trying to sell her anti-aging stuff, and so she got insulted and left. They haven't spoken since."

Mike claps his hands. "That's it! What if we pretended we were selling something?"

I consider this. "Maybe not selling, but we could pretend we are doing a project for school. Like on the funeral home or something. We can try to get Mrs. Brown alone."

"Yeah, yeah, that's good!"

"But what if Mr. Brown is home? He'd never go for it, and he's probably still mad at you for chasing him."

"What difference would that make?" Mike asks. "For all he knows, we're just the same dumb kids across the street that we've always been. Why would he ever suspect that we think something is up?"

"What *do* we think is up?"

"Simple: Mr. Brown got a new leg, and for some reason it looks kind of like your dad's."

"It looks *exactly* like my dad's. Like it could actually *be* my dad's."

"That's impossible," Mike says. "Unless . . ."

"Unless what?"

"Was your dad an organ donor?"

"How should I know?"

"He probably was—cops usually are."

"Stop me if I'm wrong, Science Boy, but even if he *was* an organ donor, a leg isn't an organ."

Mike tugs his hat lower over his eyes. "I know that. I was just thinking there might be some similar donor thing for limbs—you know, for transplants. If there is, that might explain how Brown ended up with your dad's leg."

"And if there's not?" I challenge.

"Then there's another logical explanation."

"What if they're Frankensteins?" I ask, suddenly breathless, my fingertips buzzing with the idea. "What if they're stealing body parts and sewing them on themselves? You know, like an upgrade?"

"Jeez, Parker," Mike balks. "In two days you've gone from vampires, to aliens, to ghosts, to Frankenstein—"

"Think about it," I urge, gripping his arm. "That would explain how all of them seem kind of immortal."

"Hey, I never said anything about them being immortal."

"But face it, something's *off.*"

"I know, Parker. That's why I'm helping you."

I release his arm and flash him a narrow look. "Except you don't believe me. You don't think that something supernatural could be causing all of this?"

"No, I don't." He shrugs. "But I still want to find out the truth."

We turn onto Goodie Lane and come face-to-face with the ominous row of colorful, pointy houses. Mr. Marshall is kneeling in his corner yard, tending to his prize tomato plants like he does every day. He's the only one of the Oldies who doesn't have a yard full of roses.

"Right," I finally answer. I look at Mike. "So when do we start?"

"How about Saturday? We can go over in the morning before the funeral home opens and when Mr. Brown is on his run. We can figure out what we want to say when we walk home from practice tomorrow."

"OK. I can write up some fake questions to ask Mrs. Brown. I still think we should go to the library, though."

"Oh, fine, whatever. If you really want to, we can go this weekend, too."

"Saturday?"

"It's a date." He smiles. "Well, not a *date*-date. You know what I mean."

I do know what he means, but that doesn't stop my heart from beating faster. I give a cool nod and breathe, "See you" as I dart over to my house.

CHAPTER 6

It's kind of fun to have a secret, or in my case, *multiple* secrets. This thing I have going with Mike stems from something dark and unnatural and quite possibly isn't even based in reality, but it *is* a *thing*, nonetheless, and because of this we have been spending time together. Lots of time, actually. So much that even though Zoe seemed to be excited about my fake romance at first, she's now starting to get a bit jealous.

"Want to come over after school?" she asked yesterday. "Our show is on tonight. My mom can order us a pizza."

"I have track," I told her.

"After track?"

"I already told Mike I would hang out with him."

"So it's like that," she huffed, not speaking to me for the rest of lunch.

Mike hasn't helped my case at all. He walks me to the classes that I usually walk to with Zoe and sends me texts throughout the day. Everything is in code, of course, so that if Zoe snatches my phone again she can't decipher what we're talking about. Usually Mike just gives me a rundown on who he spied on that morning, since Mom is still banning me from my pre-practice runs.

"But I'll drink water!" I keep promising.

"No, Quinnie. Not when it's this hot outside."

"If I don't run twice a day, then Jess will beat my times."

"Your health is more important than your run times."

But Dad would have cared about both! I wanted to say— wanted to say but didn't, because no matter how mad I was, I couldn't risk making Mom cry.

So instead I have to rely on Mike and his watered-down intel. For instance, he'll give me the lowdown on what Ms. Bea was wearing, and especially any info on Mr. Brown. We've both been tracking Mr. Brown's run times and trying to snap as many pictures of his/my dad's scar as possible with our phones. What exactly we plan to do with all of this information is unclear, but it still seems important to gather, and it has kind of made the end of the school year seem more exciting—like I now have something to look forward to, creepy or not, instead of the usual quizzes and tests.

"Hey, Parker," Mike calls to me in science class. "Want to be my lab partner? Mrs. Carey is letting us switch."

I hesitate and flash my friend Kaylee a *Sorry* look. We've been lab partners for most of the year. "Do you mind just this once?" I ask her, feeling sick at my own words. Out of my entire friend group, Kaylee is by far the most sensitive.

She bows her head slightly and fixes her glasses. "Sure."

"It's really just for today," I promise.

She shrugs and walks to a different lab station without a word. I know I'm going to hear about it at lunch, if not from Kaylee herself, then definitely from Zoe and Lex.

"This better be important," I hiss at Mike as he pulls our Chromebook across the lab table.

"Science is very important," he says matter-of-factly, although I can see the tiny smirk forming in the corners of his mouth. "Here, read the directions." He pushes a piece of paper toward me that contains the typed-out directions from Mrs. Carey.

I sigh and read out the few lines, which explain that we're doing a virtual lab today. "Eww," I say with a shudder. "We're supposed to perform a heart transplant—*three* of them."

Mike's eyes light up. "Cool! Like cartoon ones?"

"No," I say sarcastically. "Real ones. We're surgeons now, didn't you know?"

He nudges me in the arm and logs in to the virtual

operating room by following the instructions on the paper. Mrs. Carey weaves in between our lab stations, making sure that we are all logged in to the correct site.

"Use your notes from class," she encourages. "Make sure you actually agree on a hypothesis before you begin the surgery."

She continues to talk and float around the room. I notice that Mike is already writing down a hypothesis on our lab report.

"Hey," I tell him. "Mrs. Carey said we're supposed to discuss this stuff."

"What's the point? We're never going to agree." He grins at me. "And we both know that I'm going to be right."

I fold my arms across my chest. "Are you talking about our hypothesis for this lab?" I lower my voice. "Or our other investigation?"

Mike continues to write, not even glancing up in my direction. "All of the above."

A wave of heat trickles across my skin. "If you're *so* confident, why don't you put your money where your mouth is?"

This gets his attention. "What are you talking about?"

I lean in close to him, forcing him to fully meet my gaze. "Let's make our hypothesis right now. Whoever turns out to be right—or at least the closest to being right—gets milkshakes from Harvey's for a month."

He laughs. "You're going down, Parker."

"We'll see," I say. "What's your hypothesis about the Oldies?"

"Simple. They're having some kind of surgery to stay young." He scrunches up his face. "Well, young*er*." He raises his eyebrows. "Now you."

"Simple: Frankensteins."

"Final answer?"

"Final answer."

Mike laughs so hard that Mrs. Carey shushes him from across the room. "Man, Parker," he says, "you're going to owe me so many milkshakes. Just remember that I like extra whipped cream on top."

"You wish."

"Am I going to have to separate you?" Mrs. Carey asks, suddenly at our table with her hands on her hips.

"Sorry, Mrs. Carey."

"No, Mrs. Carey."

"All right, then," she says. "Get operating!"

With this, Mike and I exchange looks before officially starting the lab.

"I can't believe you actually ditched Kaylee for *Mike Warren*," Zoe moans next period at lunch. "Seriously, what's going on? Just because you have a boyfriend doesn't mean you can't hang out with your friends."

I don't know how to respond, so instead I pretend to be really interested in Lex's new haircut, a punkish pixie cut that not too many girls could pull off.

"You're changing the subject," Zoe points out, but there's no stopping Lex once she's talking about herself. Zoe stays silent and sulks throughout the rest of lunch. The freeze-out continues through last period, where she refuses to speak to me except for the occasional one-word answer.

"You can't *not* talk to me, Zoe," I tell her after class. "This is stupid. Please don't be mad."

"Who's mad? I'm not mad. Are you mad?"

I shift my weight, then ask, "Want to hang out after practice?"

"I think I'm busy. Besides, won't you be with Mike?" She doesn't give me a chance to answer before she storms off toward her locker.

My heart sinks into my stomach. This investigation is really starting to mess things up. But I can't give in. I can't tell Zoe the truth, at least not yet. I don't follow her. Instead, I hoof it down to the field house alone.

Coach is still making Jess and me race against each other. I'm really hoping that today will be the last day of his torture. No such luck. Fridays are usually short and sweet, but Coach keeps us for the full time today, complaining that our times are inconsistent: my times today are lower than yesterday, and Jess's are higher.

"Nice job," she says, offering me a smug smile as she makes her way off the track.

I dig my heels into the ground, thinking that it would be a whole lot easier to focus if my mind wasn't always with the Oldies on Goodie Lane.

At the end of practice, I duck into the field house to change. Afterward, I find Mike leaning against the fence, wearing an impatient smirk on his face. "Took you long enough."

"Whatever," I mumble. Together we make our way up the hill.

Once we are properly alone, he looks at me. "All right. Game plan."

"What are you thinking?"

"We need to time it just right. We need to get to Mrs. Brown while Mr. Brown is on his run but before she leaves to go to the Phoenix. So when Mr. Brown leaves, I'll follow him and call you when he starts to head home."

"But what am I supposed to *say* to her? 'Hi, good morning. I think your husband stole my dad's leg'? That lady is terrifying enough as it is!"

"Man, do I have to do everything?" Mike asks. "It's easy. You go up, you tell her you're doing a school project on local businesses for social studies or whatever. You ask her permission to film an interview on your phone. Then you ask her what her full name is, how long she's lived on Goodie Lane, how long she's owned the funeral parlor, what they do with the body parts, how they reassemble limbs—that kind of stuff."

"Oh yeah, brilliant idea."

"Thanks. I *am* brilliant, aren't I?"

"Seriously, though. I should start small, like with the basic stuff, right?"

"Yeah. Let her warm up to you. See how far she'll let you get."

"What do you think I'll get out of her?"

"I don't know. Maybe nothing. But they're most definitely hiding *something*. We just need them to give up a clue."

I toss and turn all night in anticipation of our investigation. Part of me is worried about going to the Browns' house. The other part of me is worried that Mike will be a no-show and I'll be left standing alone on the Browns' porch, not knowing what to do or say when Mr. Brown comes back from his run.

Sometimes when I can't sleep, I phone Grandma Jane. Dad was her son, and after he passed, she told me to call her anytime, even at two o'clock in the morning. Tonight is one of those nights.

She answers on the second ring, her voice scratchy and rough. "Hello?"

"Hi, Grandma. Did I wake you?"

"Nonsense, Quinnie. I'm always awake for you. Now let me just get my glasses." I can practically see her feeling around the top of her nightstand—her fingers skimming over a pile of old books, unlit candles, an empty mug, some colorful crystals—until finally landing on her red plastic frames. She clears her throat. "OK, that's better. How was your day?"

I lie back against my pillow, with Billy snoring at the foot of my bed. I tell Grandma Jane all about the normal stuff, the easy-to-explain stuff, like math class, and homework, and my upcoming track meet. I complain about the tension between Jess and me at practices and how Mom was working late again.

"What did you have for dinner?" Grandma Jane asks.

"Frozen pizza."

Grandma Jane scoffs. "Nope, that's not going to cut it. Not for my granddaughter. Tomorrow night I'm going to bring you homemade pot roast and biscuits. I'll make extra so that you girls can have it later in the week."

"You don't have to cook for us again, Grandma Jane," I say, but my mouth is already watering at the thought.

"And for dessert, what about my pudding cake. You like that? The one with the chocolate chips?"

"That sounds good," I tell her, smiling against my pillow.

She starts telling me about her day, about the argument she had with the woman down the street because she didn't pick up her dog's poop from Grandma Jane's front lawn, how she tried out a new scent for a batch of homemade candles, and how she won three bridge games in a row down at the senior center.

"Old Betty didn't know what hit her! You should have seen the look on her face, Quinnie, when I cleaned out all of her quarters."

I don't care what we talk about—the sound of Grandma Jane's voice makes me feel safe and warm and loved. She's been an even bigger fixture in my life since Dad died. Mom and I have both come to lean on her when we miss him the most. I think it's worse for my mom. Grandma Jane moved in with us for a few months right after it happened and still stays over every so often on weekends. More than once, I've spied Mom and Grandma Jane in the kitchen late at night, speaking softly over mugs of Grandma's special tea, which is as soothing as her voice.

Tonight is no different: the soft rambling is enough to put me to sleep with the phone still next to my ear. Mom must check on me at some point in the night, because the next morning my cell is resting on my nightstand, charging away.

I check it now, and the butterflies arrive with Mike's text: he's waiting for me outside. I double-check that my mom's still sleeping before I quietly tiptoe out of the house.

Mike's jogging in place, the usual twinkle in his eye replaced by the game face I've seen him wear so often at track meets. "You ready, Parker?"

"I guess so."

Together we hang back in my driveway, jogging in place, watching the Brown house for any sign of movement or life. At six twenty-five, Mr. Marshall steps onto his front yard, carrying his gardening supplies over to his tomato plants. He nods to us across the street, unsmiling. I force myself to wave. At exactly six thirty, Mr. Brown emerges from his side door and bolts down the middle of Goodie Lane. After a quick glance in my direction, Mike takes off after him. I grip my phone in one hand and make my way across the street.

At this moment, Ms. Bea comes out onto her porch, the pink plastic watering can dangling from her long painted fingertips. The water spills out onto the wooden steps. "It's a little early to be making house calls, isn't it, deary?"

Her sharp voice causes a ripple of ice to run up my spine. I stand up straighter but can't meet her eyes. "I'm sure she's up," I say, pressing forward. I can feel the weight of her stare as I climb the Browns' front steps.

"Whatever you're selling, she doesn't want it."

Tiny goose bumps line both of my arms despite it being practically ninety degrees, but I think about my dad, about his smile, about his leg, and about all of the secrets that he took to his grave . . . It gives me an edge.

"I'm not selling anything," I mutter. Then I exhale slowly and ring the doorbell. *Don't be scared*, I tell myself. *You're just a good little student doing a project.*

The door opens. Mrs. Brown stands before me, and I can't help but notice that both of her hands are bandaged. I force myself to look away from her hands and up at her face. I smile.

"Do you know what time it is?" she seethes.

"I told her, Ang," Ms. Bea calls from her porch. "I told her it was early."

I clear my throat and smile broader, making it so that my eyes widen, clear and innocent, unsuspecting. "I don't think we've really met. My name is Quinn Parker. I'm your neighbor from across the street. It's nice to meet you, Mrs. Brown." I hold my hand out for her to shake and hope that she doesn't notice the tremble of my fingertips.

"I know who you are," she says, ignoring my hand. "Why are you on my porch at six thirty in the morning?"

"I'm doing a school project on local businesses, and I wanted to interview you—"

"Is this some kind of joke? Off my porch! I have to get ready for work!" She starts to shoo me away.

At this point I hear the other doors open along the street, and Dr. and Mrs. Smith step onto their porch, cradling cups of coffee, while Ms. Attwood steps onto hers, agilely bending to retrieve her morning paper. All eyes are on me. Mrs. Brown starts to close her door.

"Please, Mrs. Brown." I wedge my foot in between the door and the frame. "You did my father's service last year. Officer Parker. Remember?"

Mrs. Brown pauses and looks at me. "Of course. We do everybody. We're the only—the *best* funeral home in town." She frowns thoughtfully before adding, "Scratch that. We're the best in all of Connecticut. People come from all over for our competitive rates."

I nod so hard that I get a kink in my neck. Through a wince, I smile. "That's why I would love to interview you. You guys were so great about my father's service. Everyone in town loves your work," I say. My throat feels so tight and dry as I continue to lie. "Just a few questions? I know you're busy."

Out of the corner of my eye, I can see that Ms. Bea has continued her morning ritual of watering her roses. I'm sure she's still watching us, but it appears as though her guard is down. I can feel Mrs. Brown conceding as well. Hope wells in my chest to the point where I feel as if I might burst if she doesn't say yes.

"Two minutes. That's all you get, then I have to go

to work." She folds her arms as I fumble to take out my cell phone.

"Thank you, thank you so much. Do you mind if I film you? Just for my class?"

"No. I don't want to be on camera."

"It's like a commercial," I say, thinking on my feet. "We're going to string together a commercial of all of the local businesses as our final project."

She narrows her eyes and I notice how smooth her skin is for an old lady but also caked with makeup, the plastic-looking kind that Ms. Bea wears, almost like a mask. "OK. Fine. Just the face though. But I only have a minute. Go."

Quickly I aim my phone at her and press record on the video camera. "For the record, would you please state your full name and place of business?"

"Angela Brown. Phoenix Funeral Home. We have the best rates on services in all of South Haven." She waggles a finger. "In all of Connecticut!"

"That's great. And how long has the Phoenix been in town?"

Mrs. Brown blinks. "Fifty-five years."

"And have you owned it that whole time?"

"Yes. Well, no. It's been in the family."

"And how long have you lived here in South Haven?"

"A long time."

"What about this street?"

"Since this street was here." She scratches the back of her neck and shifts her weight, suddenly looking uncomfortable. "How long is this going to take, child?"

Before I can respond, my phone starts ringing, disrupting the video. "Sorry, can you just hold on one second?"

"No," she says simply, her eyes flat. "We're more than done." She starts to back up while I answer the call: it's Mike.

"I lost him," he says, out of breath.

"What?"

"I lost him. *Abort!*"

Mrs. Brown is already back inside the house, the door closed in my face. I scramble to gather my things, but as I turn around, I see Mr. Brown running right toward me.

"Hey!" he yells. "Hey, you! Stop! Stay right there."

I don't know or care what he wants. The expression on his face tells me to run, so that's exactly what I do. I dart past Ms. Bea, who is leaning against the porch railing, an amused look on her face. I hear Mr. Brown's footsteps behind me, but I ran with my dad every morning and I remember his weakness: zigzags. I run back and forth, back and forth in short, quick sprints until I see Mr. Brown start to break. My front door is within my line of sight, but just before I'm about to make a run for it, a voice cuts across the street.

"What's going on here?" Mike's dad, Mr. Warren, asks, walking down his front steps. He wears a trendy blue suit with a burnt-orange tie, even though it's Saturday. In his hand he carries an overstuffed trash bag.

Immediately, Mr. Brown stops moving, giving me the chance to trot over to the sidewalk right in front of Mr. Warren's house. Mr. Warren smiles at me. "Morning, Quinn." He squints down Goodie Lane. "Is my son with you?"

On cue, Mike barrels down the street from the edge of the cul-de-sac, yelling, "Par-*ker!*" at the top of his lungs.

Mr. Warren drops the trash bag and moves forward, his eyes narrowed. "What in the world?"

I wave my hands at Mike, and he comes to a screeching halt about an inch away from me, nearly knocking me down.

"Michael!" Mr. Warren scolds. "Slow down. What are you doing?"

Sweat covers Mike's face and drenches the front of his T-shirt. He tries to talk but is having trouble catching his breath. "Dad," he manages to spit out. "Mr. Brown . . ."

At the mention of his name, Mr. Brown takes a step toward us and lets out the loudest belly laugh that I've ever heard. The sound startles everyone on the street, even the other Oldies, who all turn to watch the show.

"Brian!" Mr. Brown says, stretching his plastic face into a smile so wide that it makes him look like the Grinch right before he stole Christmas. He reaches out and clutches my shoulder with one hand and Mike's with the other. His fingers feel as cold as ice, sending a chill throughout my entire body, and I want nothing more than to wiggle out from under their grip. "The kids and I were just doing some drills together. Isn't that right?" His fingernails dig into my skin.

"Keeping you young, Mr. Brown?" Mr. Warren asks with a smile.

Mr. Brown laughs again. "That's right, Brian." He lets go of our shoulders, and Mike and I both jump back behind Mr. Warren.

"How is the new wing of the library?" Mr. Brown asks, his voice low and sweet, his eyes soft and fixed on Mr. Warren as if he really cares about the answer to his question.

"Incredible, just incredible. The students, the faculty, we're all so grateful for your donation," Mr. Warren says. "For *all* of the donations that you've contributed over the years. Honestly, without your support, South Haven College would still be stuck in the Stone Age."

Both men laugh. Mike and I exchange looks. I nudge him with my sneaker.

"Dad, I—"

Mr. Warren waves him off, before motioning to the bag of trash at his feet. "Weren't you supposed to take this out last night?" he asks, his tone switching from Appreciative College President to Frustrated Father.

"I forgot," Mike admits. "But, Dad, I have to tell you something—"

"Kids," Mr. Brown interrupts. "They'll learn one day, won't they, Brian?" He sets his eyes on me. "They always learn their lesson in the end."

"That's the hope, Mr. Brown." Mr. Warren smiles before turning to us. "Come on, you two. Go get yourselves inside in the air-conditioning. You look like you're melting." He nods to our neighbor. "See you soon, Mr. Brown. And thanks again. Really."

Mr. Brown waves to us as if in slow motion, the Cheshire cat smile still plastered on his lips. "My pleasure."

Mr. Warren drops the trash into the garbage bin with a thud, then steers us up the sidewalk. "You want to come in for breakfast, Quinn? I make a pretty mean egg and sausage burrito."

"That sounds good, Mr. Warren, but I already ate," I lie, making my way to my front steps. "Thanks, though. I'll see you later." And with one last look toward Mike, I retreat into my house, double-locking the door behind me.

Immediately I run to the living room window and watch Mr. Brown walk back to his front porch. Billy is at my side, alert. I text Mike: **What HAPPENED??**

I'm sorry! he writes back. *I was behind him the whole time and then he just BOLTED! I couldn't find him anywhere. I tried to warn you . . .*

After he was already on the street!

I said I'm sorry!

I take a deep breath and squint toward Goodie Lane. All of the Oldies have disappeared into their homes, doing who knows what.

What was up with your dad? I type.

Mike sends back a money sign before writing: **The Oldies donated a ton of money to the college. Mom and Dad love them for it.**

My heart sinks. **So they won't help us.**

Nope. It's just you and me, Parker.

I look down at my phone and remember the video of Mrs. Brown. **We should meet later,** I type. **At the library.**

Ugh. I hate the library, Mike writes. **It smells weird and they don't let you eat chips.**

Too bad. I did your plan, now it's my turn. Meet me there at 3. That should give the Oldies time to cool off.

Fine. Later, Parker.

My fingers tingle as I toss my phone on the couch. Is this really my life right now? Running away from old people and snooping around with a cute boy from school? I shake my head—*Not cute, not* really *cute* . . .

Billy nudges the back of my knee with his nose, and I collapse onto the couch so that I can pet him.

"Good boy."

I hear my mom rustling upstairs and realize that I'm sitting on the sofa in a sweat-stained tank top, hugging a notebook containing field notes about our neighbors. I run upstairs to shower and lock myself in my bedroom: I need to plan.

But Mom has other ideas, and none of them consist of giving me time alone to scheme. Instead, she makes me run a bunch of errands with her, which I guess is a good thing because it means that I don't have much time left to hang around the house, just waiting for three o'clock to arrive. Mike texted me earlier saying that he can't walk over to the library with me because he's getting a ride with his mom. I suspect he's gotten dragged around on weekend errands, too. I tell myself it's fine. It's just business anyway. But there's this annoying little twitch in my stomach that I can't seem to shake as I pack my supplies and head for the door.

Mom stops me in the hallway. "Where are you going?"

"Library."

"Since when do you study on a Saturday?"

"End-of-year project," I lie. "I just want to get it out of the way before the big track meet."

Mom reaches out to brush a stray strand of hair out of my face. "My smart girl. Are you going to Zoe's after?"

Guiltily, I nod.

"OK, well don't be out too late. I'm working the night shift, so try to get a ride from Zoe's mom if you can. Mrs. Warren told me she saw strange lights coming from near the pond when she was coming home last night. I'm sure it's just kids, but still, I'd feel better if you can get a ride. And then call me so I know you're home."

"I know, Mom."

Her eyes soften as she runs a hand through the end of my ponytail. "OK. I love you. See you later. And tomorrow's my day off, so don't make plans!"

"Sure," I call over my shoulder as I'm halfway out the door.

CHAPTER 7

The quickest path to the library would be to cut past the pond, so even though my mom told me to stick to Main Street, I head down toward the edge of the cul-de-sac.

There's no sign of life at any of the Oldies' houses, but I keep my pace steady, not too slow, not too fast. It feels strange to break through these woods without running. It feels even stranger to see the pond alone—without Mike, without anyone.

The pond itself is still. The curtain of trees creates a canopy of branches that litter their leaves all over the algae, making the water look solid on top. I can't decide if the effect is beautiful or creepy or something in between.

I pick up the pace. I want to stay close to the trees and

keep my distance from the water. But my feet have other plans: they trudge across the soggy earth, pulling me forward until my toes are planted at the edge of the pond. I peer down, my heart beating faster but my body unable to move.

"Quinn..."

"Who's there?" I look around the woods, trying to find whoever is calling me, but no one comes forward. I'm alone.

"Quinn..."

There it is again! A muffled human voice, calling my name. It sounds scratchy and distorted, but it's most definitely saying *Quinn.*

"Hello?" I ask, spinning around. All at once the branches seem darker and more ominous, as if at any moment they could reach out over the water and snatch me in their spiny arms. The tree at the far edge of the pond is by far the creepiest, with its scarred trunk and burnt, peeling bark. Rumor has it that it got struck by lightning. Now its limbs droop down toward the water as if it's sleeping and waiting for someone to wake it back up.

The water! Just below the roots of the lightning tree, a soft orange light emanates from the pond. I think back to the other day when Mr. Brown zoomed past Mike and me. I saw something that day—a glimmer of orange below the surface, but not nearly as bright as this. What *is* it? Some kind of weird, fluorescent fish? Or algae that glows? Mike would know. Where's Science Boy when you need him? I start to follow the rocky edge all the way around until I'm right beside the lightning tree.

"*Quinn...*"

There it is again! The voice, rising up from the pond.

"*Quinn...*"

The light pulses like a heartbeat each time the water whispers my name. I search for its source, and I hear my name again, being called from below the surface. It's almost as if someone—or something—is *in* the pond. I lean in more, bit by bit... closer... closer...

Suddenly a dog barks in the distance, loud enough to shake me back into the moment. When I look down, I see my toes hovering over the water. One more step and I would be under, swallowing algae. The dog continues to bark, and it's the motivation that I need. I run as fast as I can. I dart past the pond, past the lightning tree, which seems to turn and watch me as I move. I keep running until I'm through the other side and out onto Main Street.

I only stop running when I see a group of kids sitting in front of the convenience store, passing a bag of chips between them as they argue about something that sounds like Dungeons and Dragons. I think I recognize them from school. One of the girls smiles at me, setting my body slightly at ease, even though I still feel cold all over, and my head is starting to ache.

What *was* that? What happened back there? I must be

imagining things. Mom said that dehydration has some wild side effects—maybe I just need a glass of water. Maybe I didn't see what I thought I saw. Or hear what I heard.

I shake out my limbs as I push forward on the sidewalk. *It was nothing. It had to be nothing.* I keep walking, slowing down my breaths with each step.

But once the tingling in my hands starts to fade and the sunshine brings back some much-needed warmth to my body, I can't help but wonder, *What if it wasn't nothing? What if it was a clue?*

One thing's for sure: I need to talk to Mike.

The library is only about a mile away, so I pick up the pace. My brain is bursting with questions that I need to find answers to: What's really going on in South Haven, and why are Mike and I the only two people who seem to think that something's wrong? How is all—or any—of this possible?

I make my way through downtown. South Haven is located on the shoreline, and you can smell the sea from Main Street. I breathe in the salty air as I pass by my favorite ice cream place, Harvey's, which is crowded as usual, with music blaring through the outdoor speakers. I spot a couple of kids from school and I wave hi as they call out to me.

"Hey, Quinn. Come sit with us," Philippa Dash says, motioning for me to join her table.

A slight pang hits me in the gut as I smile back and

hover on the sidewalk. Part of me envies them and the blissful way they can sit and laugh and eat ice cream, without a care or a worry about what's happening just a few streets over. I can't help but think about all of my unanswered texts from Zoe and the girls, not to mention all of the hangouts that I've been missing because of this investigation. *A means to an end,* Mike had said. And he's right: this is all for the greater good. We need to figure out what's going on. What if the Oldies' plan is to hurt someone? What if it's something horrible and Mike and I are the only ones who can keep the town safe?

"Sorry, I can't. Maybe later." And with one last wave, I keep walking.

Mike is sitting on the rail of the library stairs. His hat is pushed down so low over his eyes that he doesn't see me yet. I sneak up behind him and swipe his hat.

"Parker! Hey, give it back." He's quicker than I am, and I don't try that hard anyway, so he gets it back within seconds and pulls it over his head.

"That was for this morning."

"Hey, I said I was sorry."

"He *chased* me."

"And you got away. I guess you're faster under pressure."

"Except I think they might be onto us."

Mike laughs. "Onto us? For what? Being at his house?"

"You don't think so?"

"Nah! They don't know anything."

"Then why did he chase me?" I demand.

Mike shrugs. "He's a weirdo. They're all a bunch of weirdos."

"I don't know . . ."

"You said exactly what I told you to say, right?"

"Yeah. I filmed it all on my phone."

"What did you film?" asks a familiar female voice behind me.

I spin around and come face-to-face with Zoe. Shocked, I jump back and step on Mike's foot, and he lets out a yelp.

"What are you doing here?" I ask.

"I'm on my way to my piano lesson." She tucks her skateboard under her arm and cocks her head to the side. "What are you doing? A haunted library is a weird place to go on a date."

"The library's not haunted," Mike says.

"Sure it is," Zoe insists. "There's a ghost woman in the stacks."

I know what she's referring to: the ghost of an executed witch floats between the shelves, but nobody I know has ever seen her. Legend has it, her doomed trial went down next door in the Town Hall.

"Definitely not haunted," Mike says.

"Fine," Zoe says, shifting her weight. "The not-haunted library is a weird place to go on a date."

I feel my cheeks growing hot. "It's not a date."

Mike clears his throat, reminding me about our fake romance. I can feel myself sweating. "I mean, it *is* a date. A science date."

Zoe crinkles her nose. "Science?"

Mike blinks at my pathetic lie before jumping in. "Yeah, I'm helping her," he explains. "She's, like, *failing*."

At this, I want to smack him in the face with his own hat.

Zoe's eyes widen. "You're failing, Quinn? I thought that was impossible with Mrs. Carey. She's like the easiest grader ever." Suddenly her expression changes, and she lets the hair fall over her face, hiding her eyes, something she always does when her feelings are hurt. "Why didn't you tell me? I could have helped you. I'm OK in science."

"I'm not really failing," I stumble, shaking my head. "He's exaggerating."

"No, I'm not. She's got a big old F." He pretends to draw an F in the air with his pointer finger.

I elbow him in the ribs before turning my biggest smile on to Zoe. "Yeah, so I guess we should go get to it," I say, nodding to the library behind us.

Zoe still looks kind of skeptical, but eventually she shrugs and drops her board back down onto the sidewalk with a thud. "Text me later," she says, and I promise her that I will as she skates off down the street.

Mike sweeps some imaginary dust off of his shoulder. "You're welcome." He starts to walk up the stairs. "Come on, Parker. We have work to do, you know."

I stomp after him, grumbling along the way. "You didn't have to tell such a big lie."

"Of course I did. Now she'll leave us alone."

"I don't like lying to my friends. And this is the second one in the span of a few days!"

"Well, too bad," Mike says matter-of-factly. "It's for the greater good—like something Batman would do."

"What are you talking about?"

"Batman gave up a lot of friends for the greater good—you know, to help his city. Don't you ever go to the movies?"

I look down at my sneakers. "Sometimes."

"I'll take you, Parker. You know, after we solve this case and I win my month of milkshakes." He winks at me, and I whack him in the arm.

Together we steer into the library and make our way to one of the private study rooms. Mike reaches his hand out.

"Let me see the video."

"What video?"

"The one you took of Mrs. Brown."

I hand him my phone. "It's not much."

I lean over his shoulder and together we watch the footage. The camera on my phone is pretty good, and it captured the tautness in her skin. And the more specific my questions got, the more uncomfortable she looked.

Mike hands the phone back to me. "Not bad, Parker. You got her to squirm a little."

"Is that a good thing?"

"It shows that she's hiding something."

"Yeah, but we already *knew* that."

Mike leans back in his chair. "So what now. Where do we start?"

"I think we should try and find records for the Oldies. We want to see if Mrs. Brown's dates check out." I wait a beat before adding, "And the pond. We need to find out what's in there."

"That's easy: *water.*"

"You're impossible. Let's just do this."

Mike makes a face. "I still think we need to do something more hardcore, like break into one of their houses."

"I'm not even going to talk about that. We're here for research. Aren't you supposed to *like* research; you know, since you're so into science?"

"Not on a Saturday—"

"Stop whining and search."

He turns to a corner computer and begins navigating toward the periodicals section of the library website. I pull up the chair beside him and watch him type in our street and town. Over one thousand results pop up on the screen.

"Narrow it down by date."

"What date?"

"Try 1965."

"Random."

"Well, that was the year Mrs. Brown said the Phoenix opened. She said fifty-five years ago."

Mike smiles at me. "Aww, there you go! I like your detective work, Parker." He types it in. The results narrow down to about two hundred. "Bam! Let's see what we got. Here, get in closer so you can see." He tugs at my chair to pull me in so that our shoulders are practically touching.

Focus, I tell myself. I read some of the headlines out loud: "New Funeral Home Opens as Two Others Close Their Doors. The Phoenix Sets the Competition on Fire." I look up. "Don't you think that's weird?"

"What?"

"The same week the Phoenix opened, all of the other funeral homes in town went out of business. I mean, it's almost like the Browns planned it or something."

"Here, check out the picture," Mike says. He reaches over to point to the screen, and in doing so, touches the side of his knee to mine. I clear my throat and try not to move as I follow his gaze. Front and center below the first headline is a photograph of the Phoenix during what looks to be the groundbreaking ceremony. Mr. and Mrs. Brown stand behind the ribbon, holding a pair of oversized scissors.

They look more or less the same as they do today, over five decades later.

"They don't *age*," I gasp. "I mean, I'm no math genius, but shouldn't they be hitting ninety or something now?"

Mike shrugs. "Could be relatives. Sometimes family members just look alike. My mom is always telling me that I'm my uncle Joey's twin."

"This isn't the same thing and you know it," I argue. "Look: they are *exactly* the same. Don't you get it? These are the Oldies, the same ones living across the street from us. I'm telling you, they're immortal."

"Why are you so set on the Oldies being something supernatural?" he asks. "The most logical explanation is that they've had a surgery—or maybe a lot of surgeries."

"I just have a feeling," I insist. "And my dad taught me to follow my instincts. He thought they were inhuman, too. He just never figured out how. Or what . . ."

At the mention of my dad, Mike's face softens. "Let's just keep looking." He continues typing, and I listen to the sound of his fingers tapping along the keys. Suddenly he leans forward.

"What?" I ask. "You found something?"

"Look." He points to the screen. "Mary Hove lived in your house—you know, the girl who drowned in the pond. She was the last one to live there until you guys moved in. In between, the house just sat empty."

"What about your house?" I ask, leaning forward. "Was yours empty, too, before you moved in?"

"Nope," Mike says. "There have been a bunch of families in and out of ours. No one really stayed for more than a few years. But no records of anyone else in the Oldies' houses at all, or yours." He clicks out of the records document and opens up one of the articles.

I inhale deeply and examine the picture above the new page. "Except for Mary Hove."

"I always thought she lived over by Judson. Isn't that where the dedication plaque is?"

"Yeah, but according to the *South Haven Times*, that's where her parents and little brother moved to *after* the accident. But my house"—I point to the article—"is where she lived up until she died. Don't you think that's strange?"

"Coincidental, not strange."

It suddenly feels very cold in the library, as though someone just cranked up the air-conditioning. I stare at the picture at the top of the page: a school photo of Mary Hove, her dark brown hair pinned back neatly, her smile serene. I think about her drowning in the pond, the same pond that beckoned me toward it just an hour earlier. Could there be a connection? Could Mary Hove be trying to give me a clue? Or a warning?

"Let me try something," Mike says. He clicks away for a few moments, until hitting on something that makes him perk up. "It says here that the houses on Goodie Lane were built in 1878. Look! Those five houses have been owned by the same five families since these records started."

"But it's not the same five *families*," I tell him, "it's the same five *people*. Look! It says that Jonathon Brown owned house number four on Goodie Lane in 1878 . . . in 1978 . . . in 2008 . . . all the way to now." I grab his arm. "You *so* owe me a milkshake!"

Mike frowns at me. "What if it's just a family name? You know, like all of the men are named Jonathon or something?"

I eye him. "*All* of the Oldies have family names? No way. This proves it. This proves that they're the same people. Their ancestors never owned the houses like everyone always thought; it's been *them* the whole time."

"But *how*?" Mike asks. "And what in the world does this have to do with Mary Hove? Why is her info mixed with all this stuff about the Oldies? It's like they're connected or something."

I feel almost as dizzy as I did the day that I collapsed on the track. "Mike, the *leg*."

He looks at me. "What about it?"

"Look, I don't know anything about a connection between Mary Hove and the pond, but think about it—I mean, one Oldie works with makeup, two work with dead bodies, I'm sure the others do something useful . . ."

"What are you saying?" he asks.

"The same thing I've *been* saying: they're using fresh body parts to stay alive. They're upgrading." At this I jump to my feet. "Ha! I *told* you! You owe me a milkshake!"

"Calm down, Parker." He waves me off. "We need a lot more proof before I buy anyone a milkshake."

A knock at the door interrupts us as a librarian pokes her head into the room. She smiles.

"Excuse me, kids. Are you about finished with this room? This man has it reserved for four o'clock." She gestures to the man standing beside her and I gasp: it's Mr. Marshall! He eyes the computer screen behind us, and I scramble to close out of our search and delete the history. Mike and I then collect our things and file out, not looking at Mr. Marshall as we walk by. We stop briefly in the lobby.

"Did you see that?" I cry. "I told you they're on to us!"

"Don't be so paranoid," Mike says. "It's just a coincidence. *Public* library, remember?"

I feel like I'm melting as we step into the hot sun. Mike pulls his hat down lower over his eyes, and together we begin to walk, taking the long way home, avoiding the pond.

"I'll text you later," he tells me, stopping on the edge of the street.

I take a long look across Goodie Lane. Our neighbors' houses look quiet and still. I wonder where they all are. I wonder what they're doing, what they're thinking, what they're plotting.

I nod to Mike before spinning around and heading toward my house. Relief washes over me when I notice Grandma Jane's car parked in the driveway.

I find her waiting in my kitchen with about a pound of crystals hanging from her neck, along with a warm smile and some pot roast.

"Hiya, kiddo," she says, pulling me tightly to her chest. She smells like oils and herbs.

"What are you doing here?" Mom asks from behind. "I thought you had plans with Zoe."

"We already hung out," I lie, feeling myself blush. I study Mom's street clothes. "What are *you* doing home? I thought you had a night shift?"

"I was double-scheduled with Megan, so I got sent home." She smiles. "Now we get to eat together." With this, she hands me a stack of four plates. "Can you set the table, honey?"

I squint at the dinnerware and ask, "Why four?"

"Uncle Jack's joining us. Grandma Jane ran into him on her way over."

I grin. Uncle Jack isn't really my uncle. He was my dad's best friend since they were kids, and they were partners on the force. He still pops in every now and then to check on Mom and me. He's got this big barrel chest and a mountain-man beard that he grows extra-long in the winter. He's kind of the opposite of my dad—Dad was really healthy and into running and into *playing* sports, whereas Uncle Jack prefers greasy food and *watching* sports.

As if on cue, the doorbell rings.

"I can smell the pot roast from here!" Billy starts to run in circles at the sound of Uncle Jack's voice; he loves Uncle Jack almost as much as he loved my dad.

"Just in time, Jack," Grandma Jane says.

"I'm always on time for food. It's a gift." He hands Grandma Jane a baguette as he kisses her on the cheek. Grandma Jane, in turn, hands him a soda. "Hey!" he cries, stooping to pet a very excited Billy. "How's my best bud doing? You're getting too skinny. Are they feeding you?" He lets Billy lick his face before standing back up and crossing over toward me.

"What's happening, Quinnie?" He pulls me in for a tight bear hug and ruffles my hair just like he used to when I was little. I squirm and pretend to hate it until he releases me. He then goes and does the same thing to my mom, who playfully socks him in the stomach.

"Now, now, kids," Grandma Jane scolds. "Let's sit down and eat before it gets cold."

"Don't have to tell me twice," Uncle Jack says, pulling up a chair and cracking open his can of soda.

Grandma Jane serves us each (including Billy) a

heaping platter of meat and potatoes, which I dig into, the sauce trickling down my chin. We are all silent for a while as we eat, appreciating the good cooking—Mom is a terrible cook and Uncle Jack lives alone and survives off of cheap takeout.

"So, Quinnie, how's school going?" Uncle Jack asks with his mouth full.

I make a face. "It needs to *end.*"

Everyone laughs as though I just said something funny. "What?" I ask. "I'm serious. Even the teachers act like they don't want to be there anymore."

"What about track?" he asks. "You got any big meets coming up that I should check out?"

"The one against Bedford is soon," Mom tells him before making pointed eyes at me. "But she may not make it to the meet if she doesn't properly hydrate."

"I told her the same thing," Grandma Jane says. "Didn't I, honey?"

I pretend to be really interested in my pot roast.

"What are you talking about?" Uncle Jack asks.

"Our little track star almost fainted at practice," Mom says before I can answer for myself. "She's been running twice a day, and it's too much in this heat."

"Wait, hold up," Uncle Jack says. He takes a swig of his soda and clears his throat like he always does before he is about to say something important. "Are you telling me you got in trouble for working *too* hard?" He smacks the table. "See that? That right there is what's wrong with this country. Kids today can't win. We punish them if they're lazy. We punish them if they work too hard."

"I didn't get in *trouble*," I admit. "I just got a little dizzy, that's all."

Grandma Jane shovels more potatoes onto my plate. "What's done is done," she tells them. "Quinnie here learned her lesson, didn't you, honey?"

I nod and swallow a large bite of potato. "Sure," I say, and exchange looks with Uncle Jack.

"That's all right, kiddo," he says, nudging me in the arm with his elbow. "You'll show them all at your meet. And if you ever need a running partner, just let me know."

"You?"

He laughs. *"Psych!"* He howls at his own joke. "Seriously, though, maybe you could partner up with one of your neighbors. While on patrol this morning I saw one of them sprinting around the pond." Uncle Jack is still laughing, but I freeze with my fork in midair.

"You saw Mr. Brown?"

Uncle Jack nods. "He's a heck of a runner, that's for sure. He could outrun me, and I've got to be half his age."

"To be fair, though, anyone could outrun you," Mom jokes. Her smile warms me to my core: it's a rarity to see her laugh or joke these days, but Uncle Jack has this ability to bring it out in people.

"That hurts, you know?" He pretends to cry before drenching a hunk of bread in the gravy. Grandma Jane piles a second helping of meat onto his plate.

"Uncle Jack, what do you think about the Oldies?" I ask, trying my best to sound casual.

"Quinn, what did I tell you about calling them that?" Mom scolds.

Grandma Jane waves her away. "Oh, let her say it. They *are* old, even if they like to pretend otherwise."

"I don't really think about them, kiddo," Uncle Jack says. "They're kind of just *there*, aren't they?"

"But don't you think it's weird that no one can remember who lived in those houses before?" I press. "It's like they've been here forever."

"I don't know. This was always your dad's thing, not mine. He was convinced that there was some big mystery to them, or that they were somehow inhuman. The guys at the station used to rag on him for it, used to call him Officer Ghost Hunter." Uncle Jack laughs at the memory.

I put down my fork and lean forward. "Did he really think they were *ghosts*?" I practically whisper the last word.

"Your dad thought a lot of things," Uncle Jack says through a mouthful of meat.

"How embarrassing," Mom moans. "I told him to leave those poor people alone."

"So you don't think there's anything *off* about them?" I ask, ignoring Mom's comment.

Uncle Jack wipes his second plate clean with yet another hunk of bread. "They're nice enough," he says. "Generous, too. After we lost your dad, they donated a bunch of money to the station. Can't fault them for that, now, can we?"

"No," Mom agrees. "We definitely can't."

Grandma Jane stands up. "Well, I don't know about you all, but talking about those old bores is making me lose my appetite. And I made chocolate chip pudding cake!" She goes over to the fridge and takes out a cake frosted with layers and layers of fudge.

"Oh, Janie," Uncle Jack says, licking his lips. "I think you should just marry me right now!"

Grandma Jane laughs and whacks him in the arm. "You're so fresh, Jack. If you're not careful, I'll give you the tiniest slice." But everyone knows that's not true: she cuts the cake and gives us each a ridiculously large piece. I take a bite, and for a moment, everything feels right in the world.

I carry the feeling with me all the way until bed, when I snuggle beneath my sheets and check my phone for the first time all evening: I don't even care when I notice that my message box is empty.

CHAPTER 8

Mike Warren has gone AWOL. It's been two days since the library, and he hasn't said a word to me: no texts, no messages, no hallway chats. This morning I waved hi, and all I got in return was a half-hearted head nod as he kept rolling by.

"What's with him?" Zoe asks, frowning. "Did you two break up or something?" Her eyes widen with so much empathy and concern that it almost makes me tear up.

"No," I mutter. "Everything's fine."

She throws a look toward Mike's back. "Well, he's acting like a jerk, if you want to know the truth. Want me to yell at him for you?"

"No thanks." I stiffen and pretend not to care. Truth

is, I *do* care. He *got* me to care, to go full-throttle with this whole investigation, to wait for his text messages, to look forward to our hallway run-ins and our partnerships in science. Now it's like nothing ever happened, like we never shared a computer in the library, never chased each other down the street, never had a secret. I don't get it—he was *excited* by the research in the library. He wanted to go bigger. What happened?

At least I'm sticking with the investigation, even if it feels a little empty without my partner. I have split my time between researching Mary Hove and digging through Dad's old filing cabinets in the basement, drawer by drawer.

Yesterday Mom and I went shopping in the morning. After lunch she dropped me off at the library. I dug around in the archives for a few hours and found out that Mary's funeral was the first one that the Phoenix handled after they opened. Before then, the Browns owned a funeral home in another town, over in Trumbull, I think the article said. They were working there for years before moving the business here.

Like last time, whenever I found something new about the Oldies, I also found another reference to Mary Hove. Mike had asked about the connection between the two—if there is one—and honestly, I'm still not sure. Yes, they handled her funeral, and yes, they lived across the street from each other, but what does that *mean*? At times like this, I wish that Mike hadn't ghosted me so that we could figure it out together.

So far, Dad's filing cabinets have turned up even more dead ends.

Dad had obsessions: he obsessed over his job, he obsessed over running, he obsessed over freshly made donuts, and he obsessed over answers. The more I think about it, the more I wonder whether or not he figured out any Goodie Lane mysteries before he died and just didn't get a chance to tell anyone. The one lucky break is that Dad was kind of a pack rat—a *neat* pack rat, but a pack rat. He kept a whole row of filing cabinets in the basement. Mom and I haven't really gone through his things together yet, and the filing cabinets in the basement will be last on our priority lists when we finally start the sorting process. Mom always said that only one of the four filing cabinets holds papers of actual value, and the other three are just garbage. So far all I've found are receipts, old movie tickets, and birthday cards.

I have to be quiet as I search. Mom can't know what I'm up to. Some drawers are easier to search than others. I had to stop the other night when I came across a folder full of old drawings that I had made for Dad when I was a child. He kept every single one, be it a scribble or a comic, a made-up animal, a Christmas tree, or a stick-figure police-man. The ones that got torn he had carefully taped back together. Some of them had little Post-it notes attached to the edges, detailing when I had made each picture and for what occasion. It's times like this when it hurts so much to miss him.

But I have no choice but to keep digging—I owe it to my dad. So after practice, I grab a glass of iced tea before heading back down the musky basement stairs, Billy trotting behind me.

I stare at the narrow row of filing cabinets, noting that I'd already searched the first three, which leaves just the last big one against the wall. Billy nudges me with his nose, and it's enough to give me strength.

"Let's do it," I tell him, and we set to work—and by that I mean that I start digging while Billy takes a supportive nap in the corner.

With my headphones on and the music blaring, the searching is bearable. I quickly start to organize piles: house stuff, car stuff, work stuff. I sing softly while I shuffle and shift, knocking out the first drawer, then the second, then the third.

"Last one, bud," I tell Billy, who gives me a slight nod as if he somehow understands how important this is.

I crouch down to the concrete floor, peering inside the final drawer. I gasp, causing Billy to jump to his old feet and trot over to me. From out of the drawer I grab a handful of Dad's old casebooks, pulling them onto my lap along with

Billy's head, which is nuzzled beside them. I start flipping through one at random.

"They're all filled in," I breathe. Billy licks my hand as I turn the pages.

I skim over Dad's words, running my finger along his familiar scratchy handwriting:

February 19. A at the store with B buying 4 bottles
    peroxide.
July 5. Morning run. Saw B watching me again.
    A = bandaged. 3x lm.
August 7. Toxic smell at pond. ? S + S
November 22. B and B? Being followed during run
    by pond.
March 30. Mary Hove.
April 22. Mary Hove. ONLY TRUST RED . . .

I let out a squeal, startling Billy. "Sorry, boy," I tell him, ruffling his fur. "But don't you see what this means? Mike and I are on the right track." I stiffen as I correct myself. "*I'm* on the right track."

Billy pants back, licking my face. I feel like I can just melt into the concrete floor, in between Dad's workbench and the shelf of emergency canned goods.

This. Is. Huge.

Dad would only have kept these detailed notes if he

really suspected something. This means I'm not losing it. Or paranoid. Or just a stupid kid on some stupid investigation. This means that I'm a cop's daughter following a cop's instincts, and there's no turning back now. I have to find out the truth.

I start to gather the casebooks together into a pile, and an old newspaper clipping falls out of one of them. Carefully, I unfold the paper and read the report to myself.

Local Girl Drowns in Pond

On July 5, the body of Mary Hove was removed from the Goodie Lane pond. Mrs. Hove reported her daughter missing to police on July 4 after the 15-year-old did not come home from the town fireworks display. Foul play is not suspected: police suggest an accidental drowning. Hove's body has been released to the Phoenix Funeral Home, with private services being held on July 7.

I turn the paper over in my hand, looking for more information but finding none.

I wonder if Grandma Jane remembers anything. The drowning had to have been the talk of the town when it happened. And this many years later, kids my age still know about it and make up stories about Mary's ghost.

I reread the article again and again, and each time my eyes linger over the word *Phoenix*. If anyone knows the truth, it's the Browns. Mary Hove was their first service, after all. I don't know how, but I'm going to find out the truth, with or without the help of Mike Warren.

It's hard to focus at school that next week. Mary Hove consumes my thoughts day in and day out. I sit in class and imagine her sitting in my very seat years ago, when she was my age. I picture her neat, pinned-back hair, her white dress with the Peter Pan lace collar, legs crossed under the desk, very ladylike and proper.

Mike is still pretending that I don't exist, and unfortunately, we're stuck as lab partners: Mrs. Carey made it official yesterday. Mike leans against his lab stool with his back practically to me, just going through the motions of each lab as though we aren't actually supposed to be doing them together.

"What's *with* you two?" Zoe asks at lunch through a mouthful of lettuce. "Are you still fighting?"

"No," I say truthfully. I take a huge bite out of my sandwich. "Not fighting. Just not together." Saying it out loud hurts more than it should.

Zoe grabs my arm. "Quinn! Why didn't you tell us? I'm so sorry. What happened?"

At once, the girls crowd around me, asking for details that I don't have. I just wave them off and pick at my food, counting down the seconds until lunch is over.

"Breakup or not, he hasn't stopped staring at you since we got in here," Lex says, her eyes darting over to Mike's table. "That's the sixth time today—a new record for him!"

"I forgot you keep count," I mumble.

"I keep count every day. Just because I haven't mentioned it lately doesn't mean I haven't noticed."

"Has he been staring *more* often?" Zoe asks. Normally I would yell at her for encouraging Lex, but I have to admit, since Mike stopped speaking to me, I'm interested.

Lex nods. "Definitely. He's like a sad little puppy watching you through the window."

At this, I turn around and stare right back at Mike. I glare at him until he panics and looks away, pretending to be interested in something on his cheeseburger. The girls are hysterical.

"Did you see how scared he got?"

"That was priceless!"

Zoe, meanwhile, tears her chocolate chip cookie in half and hands me the bigger piece. I wish more than anything that I could tell her what's going on. I miss hanging out with her. I miss being and feeling normal. Mike's words ring in my ears: *You have to be like Batman; this is for the greater good.* Well, even Batman had a sidekick, right? I need to find out what's really going on with him. After practice, I will *make* him talk to me.

Practice is a bear. Coach is unrelenting despite the heat. Our last meet is right around the corner, and Coach will be scoping out captains for next year.

"Now is *not* the time to slack off, ladies and gentlemen. *Move* it! Double time!"

Jess and I are paired up again. I try three separate times to start a friendly conversation and am answered with cold silence. *Oh well*, I think. *You can't say I didn't try.* Besides, my focus is on Mike. He doesn't even glance my way, not even when we pass each other on the track. Being iced out lights a fire in my legs and I run so hard that I beat two of my best-ever times.

"That's what I like to see, Quinn," Coach praises.

We finish a few minutes late, so I bolt to the field house to grab my bag. I don't waste time changing. I want to catch Mike on his way out before he escapes.

I wait at the bottom of the hill outside of the boys' entrance, bracing myself with my lack of a plan. Finally, I see him and his stupid hat, pulled down low over his eyes. He stays huddled with his friends and pretends that he doesn't notice me when I call his name. But I step directly in front of him, blocking his path.

"Something wrong with your ears?" I ask. "Because I know nothing's wrong with your eyes. What, you can stare at me at lunch every day but not talk to me?"

"Parker, calm down—"

"I *am* calm!" I cry. People are starting to snicker, but I don't care—I can't stop myself. "You"—I poke him in his chest—"are a sorry excuse for a neighbor."

"Let's walk," he says, pulling his hat up to meet my gaze. With this, he begins making his way up the hill. I'm left staring in shock at the back of his head, but he waits for me to catch up. We continue walking in silence until we reach Main Street.

"You OK now?" he asks once we turn the corner.

"I'm fine. It's *you* that's changed." My shirt is sticking to my sweaty back, and I start to wish that I had changed, or at least toweled down. So far, the lack of an apology that I'm receiving wasn't worth rushing off the field for.

Mike sighs. "I haven't changed. I didn't bail on purpose."

I snort. "Is that a joke?"

"I got a letter."

I slow down my pace. "What kind of letter?"

"The bad kind. The threatening kind."

I gasp. "From?"

"You know who." He fiddles with the straps on his back-pack. "I mean, they didn't sign it, but it's obvious enough. It was waiting for me the day I got home from the library."

"What did it say?"

His lips purse together as if he's debating something. "I'll just show you," he mumbles, before pulling off his back-pack and unzipping the front pocket. He pinches a notecard in between his fingers, handing it to me. I read it out loud.

"*Tell your little friend Parker to stop snooping. Remember what happened to Mary Hove.*"

I shiver. "'Remember what happened to Mary Hove'? What's that supposed to mean?"

"They must know we're searching for something. Marshall must have told the others that he saw us at the library. Don't you get it? It's a warning."

I give myself a few steps in silence to absorb all of this. I feel Mike looking at me.

"Do you think we should tell the police?" His eyes are wide with alarm.

"I thought about that, but they'd never believe us," I say.

"My uncle Jack told me that my dad used to bring up his questions about the Oldies around the station, and the guys just laughed at him. They called him Officer Ghost Hunter."

Mike waits a beat before meeting my eyes. "Not even Jack believed him?"

"Nope. Not even Jack. Not to mention, he said that the Oldies donated money to the station." I poke him in the chest. "And *your* parents are in their pocket, and *my* mom is in a daze. Don't you see? We're on our own. We're the only ones who can figure this out."

"Then maybe we should stop," he says in a meek voice that I don't recognize.

"But then they win. We can't let them win! And don't you see? This *proves* that they're hiding something—something they don't want us to find out."

"Parker, this is real! We don't know what the Oldies are capable of."

"So do you believe me now?" I push. "Do you believe me that they're monsters?"

He narrows his eyebrows. "No. At least not supernatural monsters. But people can be monsters, too, Parker."

"You're just scared." I spit out the last word as if it's something bitter.

Mike puffs out his chest. "Scared? Who's scared? I was only worried about *you*."

We turn the corner of Goodie Lane and pause before

continuing. I stare down at the row of old houses and wonder if the Oldies are home, if they're watching us right now, if they really are as dangerous as Mike thinks.

"Whatever," I finally say. "I mean, do what you want to do, but I'm not going to stop investigating." I start walking toward my house. Mike hesitates for a moment but then quickly catches up.

I watch him take a deep breath before slowly exhaling. "OK," he says. "OK, you got me. I'm back in." He flashes a cheeky smile before adding, "Guess this means I'm like your protector or something. Kind of like Batman."

"You are definitely *not* Batman," I scoff. "And I don't need protection. I'm a cop's daughter, remember?" With this, I unlock my front door and slide into my house. The last thing I see is Mike's smile before I close the door behind me.

CHAPTER 9

The next morning, Mike and I pick up the investigation where we left off, and it almost feels like no time has been lost, which is probably thanks to me and my stellar detective skills.

"And then it said something about 'trust Red,'" I tell him, circling my arms above my head.

"What does that mean?" Mike asks, stretching beside me in my driveway.

I shrug before leaning over to touch the toes of my running shoes. "Don't know. But we need to find out ASAP."

"Agreed."

We both stand up, rolling our shoulders beneath the hot morning sun. I can almost hear the tick on Mike's watch jumping to six thirty, and right on cue, Ms. Bea steps out of her front door, her tall heels clacking against the concrete.

Mike lifts his hat and waves it wildly in the air. "Morning, Ms. Bea!" he calls, his smile overly friendly.

As usual, Bea scowls at him before filling her pink plastic watering can and giving some love to her roses. One by one, the other Oldies step outside, and for a moment everything seems completely normal. Almost.

"Are they staring at us more than usual?" I whisper.

Mike does a long side bend so that he's closer to me. "Kind of looks like it."

"Something feels off," I tell him.

"You want to run?"

"Yeah, let's go."

And without any discussion about route, Mike takes off down Goodie Lane, in the direction of the pond.

"Hey," I call to him, "wait up!"

He slows down slightly and the two of us fall into an even pace, feeling the weight of the Oldies' glares on our backs as we move. It feels good to run again in the morning.

We dart through the mouth of the cul-de-sac and cut across the thick cluster of trees until we're running alongside the pond. The sun casts a strange glow over the water, turning the dark ripples into an almost unnatural shade of orange. It looks warm, almost like the water has turned into fire. Something moves below the surface. I lean in closer, squinting. And slowly, a ghostly face takes shape, peering up from under the water. Its dark black hair spreads out around it like tentacles.

"Parker, what are you doing?" Mike calls, startling me back into the moment.

I hadn't even noticed that I'd stopped running.

"Look!" I cry, pointing to the water. "There's a—" But before I can finish my sentence, I notice that the face is gone. It was distorted like an overexposed photo, but I swear with every fiber of my being, it was most definitely a face. I turn to Mike. "Did you see her?"

"See who?"

"The woman in the water . . ."

Mike looks at me, concerned. "Maybe that's enough for today," he says gently. "Maybe we should just rest before the meet."

My feet feel cemented to the mud, and it takes Mike looping his arm through mine for me to finally move. Silently, I allow him to take me home. The Oldies smirk at us as we walk back onto Goodie Lane.

"Back so soon, dears?" Ms. Bea calls, raising her coffee mug in the air as if to toast us.

"Ignore her," Mike hisses, leading me to my door. "Are you OK?"

"I'm fine. I'll see you at the meet. Are your parents coming?"

He nods. "Yours?"

"Yup."

"So . . ."

"So go home, Mike," I tell him. "I'm fine. I think I just need to go back to bed for an hour. I'll be OK after that."

I smile hard enough to make him believe me, and once inside, I collapse onto the couch without even bothering to kick off my sneakers.

I can't stop thinking of the dark hair, curling out around the blurry face. And then it comes to me: Mary Hove! Her hair was dark. Maybe it is her. Maybe I was right that day at the library: maybe Mary Hove wants to tell me something.

Billy jumps up onto the couch and nuzzles his head in my lap.

"Hey, boy. What you got?" As I rub him, I feel something hard on his collar, and I notice that Grandma Jane attached one of her crystals to his tags. "Looking fancy," I tell him, before sinking back against the cushions. They smell like lavender and rosemary oils, and I smile as I picture Grandma Jane leaving little crystals and trinkets all over the house. My body melts into the pillow, suddenly exhausted with the sheer weight of being. Billy's breaths become longer and deeper, and together we fall into a deep sleep until Mom comes home.

"Quinn!" she cries. "Come on. You're going to be late! What are you wearing? Where's your uniform?"

I shoot up and join her in the wild bustle around the house, searching for and thankfully finding my uniform, my track bag, my lucky water bottle, and my phone.

Whatever funk I was in earlier has lifted, and I feel ready and focused by the time Mom drops me off at the field.

"I'll be in the stands with Mr. and Mrs. Warren, holding up embarrassing signs," Mom says with a smile.

I pretend to look annoyed as I slide out of the car, even though I secretly like having my own cheering section.

"Good luck, honey!"

"Thanks, Mom."

Up ahead I can see the Bedford school bus already parked along the side, the team warming up and trying to look fierce in their red and black uniforms.

"Yeah, they got here early. Coach is fired up," Jess says, following my gaze. "He wants everyone changed and out there ASAP." I look at her with raised eyebrows, because this is the most we've talked in a month. She smiles weakly, her eyes lowered. I take this as the only apology I need, and if I'm honest, I just don't have the energy for another nemesis this month.

I raise my hand for a high five. "Let's just kill this meet."

She high-fives me, and we make our way over to Coach together.

"Come on, ladies! Get yourselves ready and warmed up.

Bedford is already trying to psych us out. Don't even look at them. Just stay focused. Stay warm."

We take off to the side with our teammates. I give a subtle nod over to Mike, who nods back before continuing his stretching.

The stands begin to fill up with Rocky Hill's fans on the right and Bedford's fans on the left. I spot Zoe and Lex jumping up and down, sporting the school colors and cheering in unison. Beside them, my mom and Mr. and Mrs. Warren are waving their Rocky Hill banners as promised. I can't help but smile.

Focus, I tell myself. *You got this.*

Coach calls us over for a pep talk. I stare down at my sneakers while he talks, breathing in each word of encouragement until my limbs feel on fire and ready to burst. Coach leads us in our team cheer. And then we scream out "Rocky Hill!" and run forward, taking our positions over by the track.

Jess and I are in the first heat, which I'm grateful for. I need to get some of this adrenaline moving. I stare at the track ahead of me, focused on the finish line. *You got this*, I tell myself again.

The gun sounds, and we're off. I block out my surroundings as my feet hit the track with rhythmic thuds. I time my breaths with each movement, exhaling from the pit of my stomach and pushing the air out in controlled puffs. My legs start to burn as I stretch forward, trying to make my calves longer, stronger, faster. I can feel a girl to my left, huffing and puffing and wanting desperately to pass me. It's close—too close. I push with everything I have, falling toward the finish line with a Bedford girl and Jess both on my heels. I hear the Rocky Hill crowd roar. I won!

Coach pats me on the back. "Nice job, Parker. Now reset and get ready for the next one. Stay warm. You've got two more to go."

The girls high-five me on the side. I stretch my calves while watching the boys' heat. Mike is also up first in sprints. He doesn't win, but his time is still better than mine. Jess comes over to stretch with me and get ready for our next race. I feed off of her focus and energy. This is it. No distractions. Nothing but my legs, my breath, and that finish line.

We take our marks. I hear my fan club going wild in the stands, but I refuse to acknowledge them until I cross the finish line; the last thing I need to do is start laughing before I run. My feet are light and fly across the bright blue tartan. I'm counting, I'm breathing, I'm pushing, pushing, pushing . . . Jess hugs me before I even realize that I won again. This time I smile and wave to Mom and the Warrens in the stands. They're jumping up and down like fools. Zoe and Lex are a few seats away, cheering and hollering themselves silly.

Something is wrong, though. Mike is waving to me from

the sidelines, signaling me to look at something. I follow his gaze, and gasp: The Oldies are here. All of them. And they're watching me right now. They simultaneously start to slow clap in my direction, the rest of their bodies remaining rigid and stiff. In the bright sunlight they look far from human.

Mike is suddenly at my side. "Don't look at them," he whispers. "Just finish your last race. Don't let them see you're scared."

"I'm not scared," I lie. Mike squeezes my arm before moving away to get ready for his next event. I steal one last look at the bleachers to see that the Oldies are still clapping, but one of them is missing. I scan the crowd until my eyes spot Mr. Marshall, who's sitting a few rows back from the rest of the Oldies. He stares at me, but unlike his friends, he doesn't clap.

Coach breaks my trance by calling me over, expelling a long list of tips and reminders about my form for the 400-meter relay. Apparently, we're a little ahead of Bedford in terms of points, but it is still anyone's win. I force myself to ignore the stands while Coach talks. I shake out my limbs, eye up the Bedford girls, and focus on my breathing.

"We need this," Jess reminds me.

I nod but don't reply. Before I can stop myself, my eyes scan up to the Oldies' section. They're still there, still standing, still slow clapping with their hands outstretched in my direction. In monotonous, low voices they start to chant,

"Par-ker. Par-ker. Par-ker..." I jump backward, knocking into Jess.

"Whoa, you OK?" she asks, rubbing her arm.

"Sorry, I..." I exhale deeply through my nose and slow my breathing. "Do you see anything weird in the stands?" I'm praying that she says *nothing*, that the Oldies are just a figment of my imagination.

Jess scans the crowd. "I see your mom and the Warrens, going wild as usual. Oh, there's Zoe and Lex." She waves to them and smiles. "And there are your creepy old neighbors, chanting your name. Is that what you mean by weird?"

"Yes," I say, suddenly feeling dizzy and overheated.

"Coach says they're donors. If this meet goes well, they might give money to the team." She bites her lip. "No pressure, though. I don't want to psych you out."

I don't answer, and instead I bend over my knees, taking breaths so deep that they hurt.

Jess looks from me to the Oldies and frowns. She comes in close, gripping my shoulders. "Listen. Don't let them mess with your game. We have one more relay, one more and we beat Bedford. Just pretend they aren't there. Shift your focus." She points toward my Mom and friends, and I lock eyes with Zoe just as she cheers my name with the biggest grin on her face. It's enough.

"Come on," Jess urges, pulling me up. "Stay warm with me."

I bounce around alongside her, shaking out the nerves from my limbs, and it works. It totally works. By the time I'm called up to the track, I'm focused. I suddenly *really* want this last win. I can taste the salt on my tongue and feel the burn throughout my calves as my heart beats faster and faster. I don't look anywhere except at my target: Jess. All I have to do is catch the baton from Kaylee, pass it to Jess, and watch Jess bring it home. Nothing else matters right now except that baton and that thick white line. *Nothing.*

The gun sounds. I bob up and down, half-turned to see the progress of my teammates. I count in my head. I pace my steps and stay loose until it is time to reach and run. Kaylee's pass is timed perfectly. I'm off! I can feel the other girls behind me, but I just keep pounding forward until the baton is safely in Jess's hand. I stop, catch my breath, and watch her cross the finish line first.

I scream. Everyone screams. We huddle together despite the heat, jumping up and down in unison. The meet isn't over, but we already know we've won—it's just the icing on the cake when the officials finally announce Rocky Hill's victory over Bedford. Mike is by my side for the announcement, and he hugs me tightly in front of everyone.

I wish Dad was here. He lived for meets like this, when it's neck and neck and down to the last run. He would have screamed himself hoarse.

Coach has us line up and shake hands with the Bedford kids. Some of the Bedford girls are crying. I'm sincere, though, when I spout out the obligatory "Good meet" line to each Bedford runner. It was a narrow win and they were some good competition. Nothing's better than winning against a really good team.

Afterward, Coach pulls us in for his end-of-meet speech. "I'm really proud of you all today," he says. "I saw teamwork. I saw hustle. I saw heart." He points his clipboard at Jess and me. "I saw leadership."

Kaylee high-fives me and I can't hold back my smile.

Coach nods. "That's right. You should all be proud of yourselves. Because not only did you impress me, but you impressed our donors out there today, too."

I stop smiling. A chill runs down my spine as Mike looks over at me. He raises his hand.

"Coach?" he asks. "What exactly are the donors, you know, *donating*?"

"You name it!" Coach booms, slapping his clipboard against his thigh. He beams. "New uniforms, new hurdles, new shot put . . ."

He continues to list off items, but I'm no longer listening. I just continue to exchange worried looks with Mike until Coach finally releases us. I make a pit stop at the bleachers to tell my mom that I will meet her at the car after I change. She runs down the stairs and makes a fuss over me, shaking her banner over my head as Mrs. Warren takes a billion pictures. Zoe and Lex are next at my side, hugging me and congratulating me.

Without thinking, my eyes drift toward the other side of the bleachers; I gasp. The Oldies are still here. All of their eyes are on me now, blank and lifeless. Ms. Bea is the only one who smiles as she leads the rest of my neighbors in an exaggerated slow clap, their hands and arms outstretched toward me. I don't bother with the field house. I just pick up my tired legs and run. Ms. Bea's throaty laugh follows me until I turn the corner.

CHAPTER 10

"We have to talk."

It's hours after the track meet, and Mike is standing in my doorway. His hands are stuffed deep into his pockets, and there is no sign of a smirk or a smile. I cross my arms over my chest.

"What's up?" I ask.

"Can I come in?"

I hold open the door wide enough for him to slip through. Billy greets him on the inside.

"Sup, boy?" Mike drops to his knees to ruffle Billy's fur as I close the door.

I watch him wrestle with my dog in my living room, feeling shyer than I'm used to feeling when Mike and I are together.

"You want something to drink?" I ask.

Mike stands up. "I'll take milk."

"Milk?"

"Yeah, what of it? Vitamin D, right?"

"If you say so." I lead him to the kitchen, where I pour us both a glass before we take our seats across from each other at the little round table.

Mike doesn't waste any time. "So the Oldies at the track meet," he starts, as if we are already in mid-conversation.

"What about them?"

"That was another warning, except I can't figure out why."

"Because they know we're onto them."

Mike purses his lips. "But we're *not* onto them," he argues. "At least not fully. Face it, Parker, we still don't know who, or what, we're dealing with. We don't even know if they're really dangerous or not."

"If you don't think they're dangerous, why are you so scared of them?" I challenge.

"I'm not scared," Mike insists, puffing his chest out a little before taking a long drink of milk. "I'm just *cautious*."

"No, something is off about these people and you know it." I hand him a napkin. "You've got a milk mustache."

"I like it. Makes me look manly." But he wipes it off just the same.

"So what do you want to do?" I ask.

"I think we need to make some charts."

"OK, Science Boy . . ."

"Seriously. We have to start thinking like scientists, and to do that we need to put all of our evidence into one place. You got your laptop?"

I nod and stand up. "It's in my room."

Mike stands up to follow me.

I quickly raise my hand. "Nope. I'll bring it down." I take off upstairs before Mike can argue; the thought of him being in my bedroom is just too weird, and goodness knows I've got enough weirdness in my life these days.

When I return to the kitchen, we sit side by side in front of my computer and open a Word document that we title *Evidence*. Mike immediately opens his personal email and downloads a file onto my computer. Suddenly, candid pictures of the Oldies appear across the screen.

"Where did you get these?" I breathe.

He flashes a cheeky smile. "I took these after the track meet, on my way to the field house. They were so focused on you, they didn't even notice."

"Genius."

"I know."

I watch as Mike's fingers bounce across the keys, typing furiously without even having to look down. He pastes in each of the Oldies' photographs, along with some empty bullet points beneath each one. He then adds another two names: James Parker and Mary Hove.

"You have a box for my dad?" I ask, shocked.

Mike shifts. "Well, yeah. I mean, he's *involved*. Mr. Brown has a similar leg, *and* you've gone through his casebooks."

He clicks on a copy of the obituary picture of Mary Hove that we found in the library. I squint at the photograph, at her dark hair and eyes. I can't help but imagine this face staring up at me from beneath the pond's surface, and the memory makes me shiver.

"Let's do this," Mike says, before quickly copying over the information from the archives and Dad's casebooks.

- Disappeared on July 4, 1965
- Body found in pond on July 5, 1965: accidental drowning
- Fifteen years old
- Wrote for the school newspaper
- First Phoenix funeral
- Lived on Goodie Lane—Quinn's house

First I read over the information. Then I help Mike fill out the other boxes:

Ms. Bea
- Possibly the leader
- Frequently seen with bandages; last one around her head
- Owns a beauty shop in town
- Constantly watering her roses
- Led the chant at the track meet
- No family that visits

Dr. Smith
- Retired doctor of some kind
- Volunteers at the hospital
- Only wears black
- Most recent bandages were on his ears
- No family that visits

Mrs. Smith
- Retired chemist
- Volunteers at South Haven College
- Only wears black
- Most recent bandage was on her nose
- No family that visits

Ms. Attwood
- Town Hall clerk
- Seems to be especially close with Ms. Bea
- No family that visits

Mr. Brown
- Owner of the Phoenix
- Opened the Phoenix the year Mary Hove died; Mary Hove was the first funeral
- Most recently seen with bandaged leg; now has Mr. Parker's leg
- Claims scar is from a dog bite (same as Mr. Parker's)
- Housed Mr. Parker's funeral and had access to his body
- Runs daily (sometimes twice a day) and can outrun Quinn and Mike

- Yells a lot
- No family that visits

Mrs. Brown
- Owner of the Phoenix
- Most recently seen with bandaged hands
- Video evidence shows how plastic her skin looks up close
- No family that visits

Mr. Marshall
- Lives in a red house
- Takes good care of his tomato plants
- Retired landscaper
- Did not sit with other Oldies at track meet
- Spotted at the library during first day of research
- Has two children and four grandchildren that visit during the holidays

"Hmm," I say thoughtfully after reading the last line.

"What?" Mike asks.

"Mr. Marshall's seems, I don't know, *different* than the other Oldies. He doesn't seem as involved or something. And he wasn't sitting with the others at the track meet. Don't you think that's strange?"

"Kind of," Mike says. "I mean, not much of what they do

makes sense. But I do think it's weird that he's the only one of them with a family. You've seen them, right?"

"Yup. Every Christmas they show up. I think I remember seeing Vermont license plates on one of the cars, and Massachusetts plates on the other?"

Mike opens another file: the research we pulled at the library. "Here." He opens a document. "This shows the history of the Marshall house. Look, these records prove that Mr. Marshall's grandparents bought the house, then his parents took it over in the early fifties, then he lived there with his wife."

"What happened to his wife?" I ask.

"I don't know—I'm assuming she died."

"Does that record say her name?"

Mike scans the document. "Yup. Melanie Marshall."

I open another tab on the computer and start googling. Within seconds, I find her obituary. "She died of breast cancer in 1983," I read aloud. "She was survived by her husband, Bob, and two children, Emma and Cory. Services were held at the Phoenix."

"Of course they were," Mike says. "So what do we think? Is Mr. Marshall a goodie or a baddie? Is he an Oldie or just *old*?"

I consider his question as I continue to scroll through the obituary photos. I stop on a colored one of the Marshall family when their children were still small. Mr. Marshall's and his children's hair stood out: fire-red and curly. Today Mr. Marshall's hair is still curly, but there is far less of it, and the shocking red has faded to a deep gray.

"I don't know," I admit.

"Should I add a new column for him? Call it 'the not-so-creepy creeps'?"

"Or we could just call it the 'maybe' category." I drag the picture back over to the list of notes on the screen.

"So is that it?" Mike asks. "I mean, what's our next move?"

"We need to see them at work," I decide.

Mike snorts. "Working on what? Being creepy?"

"No, like their jobs."

"I'm not following you, Parker."

"Think about it," I say, my heart beating faster with excitement. "All of them are old enough to be retired, but they're still going to work every day."

"To be fair, though, some of them just volunteer . . ."

"Who cares? The point is, they're working for a reason. And it can't be for the money."

I can practically see the gears turning in Mike's brain. "Yeah, I mean, if they have enough money to buy a new library wing and sponsor a track team, then they have enough money to retire. Unless, of course, they're spending all of their cash on clothes."

"Be serious, Mike."

"I am serious. Their gear is *expensive*."

He's not wrong, but once again, not the point.

"What do you say?" I ask. "You in for a little spying?"

Mike grins back at me. "Always."

The next morning, I spring out of bed before my alarm clock even goes off. I'm more than ready to set our plan into motion. Only, when I look out my window, I notice that it's pouring, like *really* pouring. *Darn it.* I grab my phone and text Mike.

It's raining. You still in?

Mike writes back immediately: **Yeah. Why wouldn't I be? You afraid we'll melt?**

I make a face even though he can't see me. **Funny. Meet me outside after they leave.**

Got it, Mike writes. **I've got eyes on them now.**

I toss my phone onto my bed and start to get dressed in the clothes I laid out last night: a pair of black baggy joggers and an oversized T-shirt that I swiped from my mom's closet. They're so big that I can pull them over my normal running shorts and tank top, before zipping my raincoat over the layers. I'm sweating already, but Mike and I agreed to go as incognito as possible for some of our spy stops, specifically the Town Hall, which might not even be open given that today's Sunday.

Moving over to the mirror, I knot my hair into a bun on

the top of my head and tug my hood over it. I look equal parts sketchy and ridiculous, but at least I don't look like Quinn Parker. It'll do.

I pick up my phone and tuck it safely into my backpack, which so far just holds my wallet, a flashlight, and my water bottle. Slinging it over my shoulders, I make my way downstairs. Billy cocks his head to the side and studies me as if trying to decide whether or not I've totally lost it.

"Quite possibly," I tell him, before tossing him a biscuit.

Together we peer out the living room window, waiting for movement across the street. The Oldies usually leave around eight thirty, so if they stay on schedule, I should be able to catch them.

All of a sudden, Billy lets out a low growl beside me.

"What's up, boy?"

But I feel it, too, even before the Oldies open their doors, almost like a cold gust of air has cut across the street and through the window. I duck a bit lower. One by one, our neighbors walk out of their houses, wearing their Sunday best and carrying black umbrellas in a procession that reminds me of Dad's funeral, which was held during the thickest, coldest rainstorm. They greet one another as they gather by Mr. Brown's car. It's not exactly a hearse, but it is so long and black that it might as well be. They all manage to squeeze in without looking too uncomfortable, and then Mr. Brown slowly steers the car away from Goodie Lane.

The Eagle has landed, Mike writes.

FLOWN! I type back.

Whatever. Let's go.

I toss Billy another treat before grabbing my skateboard and making my way outside. Mike emerges from his house carrying his own board. For a moment we stand on our respective stoops, letting the rain roll off of our black hoods and listening to the sound of the water hitting the concrete. I nod once, and we meet on the sidewalk.

"I think we should cut through the woods," I tell him, motioning to the edge of the cul-de-sac. "We can carry our boards until we get to the other side. It'll save time," I add, but in truth I wouldn't mind seeing the pond again: I haven't been able to stop thinking about that face and hair spiraling to the surface.

Thunder cracks before Mike can answer, startling us both so much that we clutch our boards against our chests.

"And that's a *no*," he says, tilting his head back to the sky. "I'm pretty sure cutting through a wooded area during a thunderstorm is a bad idea."

"It's not a *storm*," I argue. "It was one little clap of thunder. Look, it's barely even raining now." It's true, the rain is subsiding a bit, but I know as well as Mike that it's probably not holding back for long.

"Let's just stick to the plan. Boards only. Skip the woods. Start with Attwood. Deal?"

I hesitate, throwing one last look toward the pond. "Deal," I mutter, and together we drop our boards and take off down the slick sidewalks until we reach Main Street.

The first stop is the Town Hall to try to catch Attwood working her magic with the Oldies' files. The building is in South Haven's historical district, only a mile or so away from Goodie Lane. Like many of the neighboring buildings, the Town Hall is an old-fashioned construction of brick and white wood, with multipaned windows and a curved bell tower at the top. Mike and I stop skating in front of the tall entrance, the bell tower illuminated against the dark gray sky. The image makes me shiver.

"What's our cover again if she spots us?" Mike asks.

"Just another school project," I say.

"You sure they're going to buy that for a second time?"

I shrug. "You got something better?"

He sighs, and we tuck our boards under our arms, making our way inside.

Mike immediately crinkles his nose. "Ugh, it smells like the *library* in here."

"Shh!" I tell him, even though he's kind of right: the lobby definitely has that musty, stale stench that reminds me of a used bookstore.

"Why are you shushing me? There's nobody here." He circles around to emphasize how alone we are.

"You're sure it's open, right?"

"Of course it's open, Parker. Why else would the door be unlocked? It's just dead."

His last words linger in my ears, and all I can do is pray that coming here wasn't a total waste of time.

"So where do we go?" I ask, spinning on the hardwood floor, listening for footsteps or voices, or a clue that we aren't the only two people here.

Mike points to a board hanging on the wall. "Here's a map. Look. Records and Archives is on the second floor." He smiles. "And the mayor's office is on the top floor. You know, if you want to go say hi and ask her opinion about the case."

"Let's just move before someone comes in and hears us."

With our hoods still on, we slink toward the far staircase, our wet sneakers squeaking against each step as we climb to the second floor.

"Check it out," Mike whispers. "There's life up here."

And he's right: the hallway is lined with offices and windows, all labeled by department, each manned by some tired-looking town worker. Regular South Haven citizens wait their turns, holding files and envelopes. I relax slightly. It feels normal—safe, even—to be around so many people. But where's Attwood?

Hugging the wall, we move past, window by window, until we come to the end of the corridor. The last window, of course, is labeled SOUTH HAVEN RECORDS AND ARCHIVES in a stick-on newspaper font. A stylish woman is on the outside of the window, wearing a short black dress with wedge sandals, her hair falling in curls down her back. As we get closer, I realize that I recognize her: it's Mrs. Massimini, the co-owner of my favorite pizza shop, Cucina Della Nonna.

Ms. Attwood pokes her plastic face through the other side of the window, smiling and nodding patiently with Mrs. Massimini. She seems so engrossed in the conversation that she doesn't notice Mike and me lurking nearby. We keep our hoods pulled down and grab a permit application from off of the FORMS counter. Holding the papers in front of our faces, we listen.

"And with the plans to renovate the restaurant," Mrs. Massimini says, "we really need to look at the original building plans."

"Of course, dear," Ms. Attwood replies with a smile. "I'm so happy to hear that you're expanding."

"Thanks in part to you and your generous donation!" Mrs. Massimini gushes.

Ms. Attwood pretends to look bashful as she waves her hand in the air. "Oh, it's nothing, dear. Really, you're doing *me* a favor. Your mother makes the best pizza in Connecticut."

Mrs. Massimini smiles. "She certainly does. And she knows it!"

At this, Ms. Attwood throws back her head and laughs a little too loudly. "Carmelina is a feisty one, isn't she?"

"You have no idea . . ."

The two continue to talk for a minute before Attwood disappears into the back to pull the paperwork. Realizing that this is our chance to leave, I motion for Mike to follow me toward the staircase. We don't talk until we reach the empty lobby.

"Well, that was a whole lot of boring," Mike moans, pulling off his hood.

"What do you mean?" I shoot back. "That was some good stuff."

"Did we eavesdrop on the same conversation? That was a dead end. We didn't even get to see Attwood messing with the records."

I wave him off. "Mrs. Massimini said that Attwood donated to the pizzeria. That's the college library, the police station, the track team, the restaurant . . . And who knows how many more? Don't you get it? They're buying their way around South Haven."

"But we already kind of knew that, Parker."

"And now we know for sure. Besides," I add, thinking back to the conversation upstairs, "didn't you notice how *good* Attwood was with Mrs. Massimini?"

"What do you mean?"

"She was nice, and helpful, and funny."

"Yeah, 'cause she's a good liar."

"Exactly!"

"But we already kind of knew that, too," Mike says.

I unzip my jacket. "*Kind of* knowing something and having more evidence are two different things," I tell him. "Weren't you the one who told me that?"

"Oh, so you *do* listen to me once in a while?" He smirks. "Let's just hope that Ms. Bea gives us something a bit more interesting."

"Agreed."

Together we pull off our black layers so that we're back in our usual running apparel and light raincoats, including, for Mike, the Yankees hat, which he seems all too thrilled to wear again. There's no point in disguising ourselves to go into our second stop: Ms. Bea's cosmetics boutique. She'll know it's us, and it will only make us look more suspicious if we wear a disguise. So instead of hiding, we're going to pretend that Mike's shopping for a birthday present for his mom. With any luck, other customers will be there, taking up Ms. Bea's time and attention.

We stuff our extra clothes into our bags and push through the heavy double doors. Outside, we drop our boards onto the sidewalk. It's still raining, but thankfully not as much as earlier. Ms. Bea's shop, La Belle Sorcière, is located on the other side of town, down by the beach. It's a long ride, but it's definitely faster by skateboard than if we were to walk. We glide through the historical district, passing by old houses with their flat fronts and iron gates, and before long we reach the streetlamp wrapped with buoys, the unofficial signal in South Haven that you're near the Long Island Sound. Ms. Bea's shop is stationed on the shore with a view of the water. It's one of three small businesses housed in a white Victorian, with navy trim and a steepled roof. There are a few cars in the parking lot: a good sign that other customers are inside.

Together, Mike and I climb the covered front steps and set our skateboards on the porch. Pushing through the front door lands us in a foyer with signs pointing to a lawyer's office upstairs and an antiques dealer downstairs, with La Belle Sorcière occupying the main floor. Pulling our hoods back, we make our way forward. We're instantly hit with the combined scents of sandalwood and rose and jasmine. Shiny tables are spread out over the dark hardwood floors: they're decorated with candles and vintage perfume bottles. Lotions and creams cover one of the walls, and an antique vanity sits in the corner, complete with a red velvet bench for customers to sit on and admire themselves in the ornate mirror. The whole room has an Old Hollywood kind of vibe, which fits with the way Ms. Bea dresses.

Ms. Bea notices us the minute we step into the space. We're dripping rainwater all over her polished floor, and her eyes narrow, following us. She's helping a young woman dressed in white choose from a selection of perfumes spread out in front of them. Another customer floats near the counter, and I'm thankful for the extra bodies in the room. Ms. Bea arches one of her penciled eyebrows.

"Can I help you?" Her voice is so smooth that the edge to it is almost undetectable.

"Just looking for a present for my mom," Mike explains. He flashes his biggest smile. "It's her birthday."

"What a thoughtful son," the lady in white says, complimenting Mike.

"Yes, how special," Ms. Bea says. She smiles back with her teeth, but her eyes don't have the twinkle that comes with a genuine warmth.

"I am pretty special," Mike tells her.

"Does this come in a bigger bottle?" another customer asks, before Ms. Bea can respond to Mike.

She throws one last look our way before turning to help the two women in front of her. Just like Attwood, Ms. Bea's manner with her customers is professional and pleasant—a wolf in sheep's clothing—that is, if the wolf had very fancy and expensive clothes.

Mike and I move over to a display of moisturizers. "What are we looking for?" he whispers, sniffing a bottle of gunk.

"Anything suspicious," I whisper back. I pick up a container and start reading the label, scanning the ingredients for any red flags. Mike follows my lead and does the same.

"You have such amazing products," one of the women is telling Ms. Bea. "They work like magic."

"Seriously!" the second woman adds. "They're like a time freeze for your face. They hide *everything*."

This all sounds like a clue. It *feels* like a clue. But looking around, there's nothing here. Just beauty products, and mirrors, and a very professional businesswoman.

More thunder rumbles in the distance.

"We'd better make this quick if we want to skate to our other two stops," Mike whispers. "The storm is definitely close."

I nod and hand him the cheapest bottle of lotion on the table. "Get this one for your mom."

"Ten bucks? Jeez, Parker, do you think I'm made of money?"

"Then you find something else. Just hurry up."

Another crack of thunder seems to shake the room, and I have the sudden urge to go home. Something feels *off* about this store, about this whole day: Attwood and Bea, carrying on as if they're not hiding something sinister. The most unnerving part about it is how *good* they are at fooling everyone.

"Fine," Mike says, taking the bottle. "I guess my mom's worth ten dollars." He trudges up to the register, where he pays with what seems to be the last of his allowance. Ms. Bea gives him a special gift box that he just shoves into his soggy backpack.

"I do hope that Mrs. Warren enjoys it," she tells Mike.

"These creams can be quite addictive, so you know where to find me if she needs more."

"Umm. Thanks. I'll tell her."

Mike and I exchange looks before scurrying out of the store, grabbing our skateboards from the porch. The rain is falling heavier now, and the ocean waves are rising and falling with such a force that I can feel each crash in my bones. I follow Mike down the sidewalk, trying my best to keep my balance as we roll past the buoys, past the old church and library, past the Town Hall, past Harvey's and Cucina Della Nonna. We don't stop until we reach the Phoenix Funeral Home.

It's a beast of a building, staged to look like an old home similar to one of the historical houses down the road. But it's a facade. The building itself isn't an original. Looking up at it now through the rain, I think about my dad's funeral service: the rain, the parade of people clad in black, the constant hugging and touching and crying. A wave of nausea rises, and instinctively, I reach for Mike's hand.

"I, I . . ." *I can't*, I want to say, but the words don't come out. Tears mix in with the raindrops, and Mike squeezes my palm. More thunder rumbles, and a flash of lightning cuts through the already-dark sky.

"Hey, it's OK," Mike says. "I think we've done enough for today."

I sniffle and nod, and together we skate home.

CHAPTER 11

I wake up the next morning surrounded by my dad's case-books. I must have fallen asleep while trying to decode Dad's notes. At least I got a little bit of shut-eye. After everything that happened yesterday, I thought I'd never fall asleep.

My head aches just thinking about it. I can't believe I froze like that, crying in front of the funeral home, squeezing Mike's hand in the rain.

Squeezing Mike's hand...

I bury my face in my pillow, hiding my blush even though no one is in the room except for Billy, who nudges his wet nose under the blanket and licks my cheek.

"Hey, boy," I say, giving him an affectionate pat on the head. "You hungry?" His old eyes widen. "OK. Let's go."

With this, I drag myself out of bed and follow Billy downstairs into the kitchen, where I pour him a bowl of kibble, and myself a bowl of cereal. We're both one bite in when suddenly there is an impatient knock at the front door. Billy and I freeze, exchanging looks. He immediately lets out a small *woof* before running for the door. I follow, stealing a peek through the side window. Mike Warren stares back at me.

"I know you're there, Parker. Let me in," he calls, tapping on the glass.

I jump back and swing the door open. "What are you doing here?"

Mike walks past me before I can even invite him inside. He looks me up and down and smirks. "Nice jammies, Parker."

Ugh! I look down in horror at my matching cupcake-printed shorts and tank top. Hastily, I snatch a hoodie left strewn across the couch and tug it on.

"Do you know what time it is?" I grumble. "We're not even running today. And my mom's still sleeping—"

"Calm down, I'll be quiet." He nods to the kitchen. "Got any cereal?"

I flash him a scowl before leading him to the table and pouring him a bowl of cereal. I then sit and watch him and Billy scarf their breakfasts until I feel like I'm going to burst. "Why are you here?"

Mike pushes his bowl away and looks at me. "You weren't answering my texts last night."

"So?"

"So I was kind of worried. You know, after—"

"I'm fine," I interrupt.

"Then why didn't you answer?"

"I was sleeping."

Mike puts down his spoon and looks at me so intently that I have to turn away. I know that he doesn't believe me, but I don't know what he wants me to say. It was bad enough that he saw me cry.

"I'm sorry I ruined our mission," I say softly. "I won't freeze next time."

Mike frowns. "Parker, that's not what I mean—that's not why I'm here. I wanted to make sure you were OK. I care about you more than the mission." He ducks his head with his last words, and I feel a flutter in my stomach.

I've never seen him like this: He looks shy. Nervous, even. My heart beats faster, and for a long moment we fidget across from each other, not knowing what to say. Billy is the first to break the silence, whining at Mike's knee. Mike bends over and drops a piece of cereal onto Billy's tongue, and the image reminds me of my dad: he was always feeding Billy table scraps. I straighten in my chair, my mind refocusing.

We still have a job to do. We have to see this mission through, no matter the cost.

An idea rushes through me, sending a buzz through my fingers. "We need Phase Two."

Mike stares at me for a beat before answering. "Phase Two of *what*?" His eyes widen. "You want to spy again?"

"Look, yesterday I froze. But today we can make it right. We can go after school. It's perfect! We don't have track and—"

"Will you slow down? I was thinking that we should lie low for a while. You know, regroup?"

I shake my head so hard that it hurts. "No. We're close, so close I can feel it. We need to keep going." I meet his eyes, pleading with him from across the table. "Please, Mike. After school?"

There is no cocky smirk when he finally nods.

School is a complete waste of time. I can't concentrate on anything except for the clock on the wall in every classroom. During lunch I just pick at my food.

"You OK?" Zoe asks, stealing one of my chips.

It takes everything for me to force a smile. "I'm good. Just tired."

"Is Mike being a jerk again?" Lex asks. "I thought you two were back together?"

"We are," I mutter. "It's not that."

Zoe leans over so that our foreheads gently touch. "Are

you missing your dad?" she whispers. "I know it must be hard, you know, hitting the one-year mark last month."

Her question shakes me. I'm not sure which affects me more: the fact that it's been over a year since I've seen my dad or that Zoe is such a good friend that she is thinking about it, too. I blink back tears, and it takes me a few full breaths before I can answer.

"I'm OK," I say, adding yet another lie to the pile.

"You know I'm here for you, right?"

I nod. All at once the sound rushes back to me, as if I'd just burst through the surface after being under-water for too long. Zoe straightens herself, taking her warmth with her. I give her the rest of my chips before the bell rings.

After school I find Mike at his locker; I hover back a bit while he says goodbye to his friends. When he sees me, he replaces his smirk with his game face.

"What's the plan, Parker?" he asks as we walk out of the building.

The humidity feels worse out here, and within two feet I'm sweating.

"You said that the Oldies are always home before three, right?"

"Right."

"So I bet that's when they're at their most relaxed," I explain. "They're probably a bit looser when they're tired after a day of work."

"You thinking they'll talk? Let some clue slip?"

"Maybe."

Mike smiles. "Hold up, though. Let me get this straight: You, a cop's daughter, want to spy through our neighbors' windows? Isn't that against the law?"

I bite my lip. "Just a *little* bit of the law. I mean, I'm not saying that we should break in or anything . . ."

"Still, Parker. This is a lot more intense than just researching in the library. I feel like I'm looking at a new you."

"Is that a bad thing?"

He grins. "Not at all."

For some reason this causes me to smile back. "So the plan is—"

"Peep through some old ladies' windows." He makes a face. "Actually, saying it out loud makes it sound *so much* worse."

I laugh. "Seriously, though, we should focus on Bea, right?"

"Not Brown?"

"No. Bea seems to be their leader. I bet she has more secrets than we know."

We continue to walk until we get to the corner of Goodie Lane; here we hesitate and look around, making sure no one else is out and about on the street. Mr. Brown's car is parked in his driveway, but the houses all look quiet.

"I think we're clear."

We walk as casually as possible down the Oldies' sidewalk.

"What do we do if they catch us?" I whisper.

"That's easy, Parker. We run."

I scan each window as we move, but no one appears to be looking out. I really hope I'm right that their guard is down at this hour.

When we near Ms. Bea's house, Mike pulls me toward the rosebushes beneath the side windows. The bushes are large enough to hide in even if it means getting a few hundred thorns in my arms.

"Ow!"

"*Shhh . . .*"

"Oh wow, look!"

Peering up, we can see straight into what appears to be Ms. Bea's living room. It's decorated in a sea of mauve and reminds me of her cosmetics store, with antiques and velvet everywhere. Above the sofa, there's a large painting of a beautiful, young woman wearing a green dress. Her eyes and hair are dark, her features angular. She looks just like a young Bea.

Ms. Bea suddenly enters the room, wheeling in a big metal suitcase. Heaving, she pulls it onto the coffee table.

My stomach drops. Mike and I duck slightly before peering in again, our fingers gripping the windowsill. A thorn tears into my thigh and I can feel a small trickle of warm blood run down my leg, but I ignore it. This is way too important.

Mrs. Smith joins Ms. Bea on the sofa. Everything they say is muffled. I can't make out a single word with the window closed. Just when I start to worry that this is going to be another dead end, Bea opens the suitcase. I squint: it appears to be just a bunch of tubes and bottles, similar to the ones she sells in her store.

"Oh great, we've arrived in time for makeovers," Mike whispers dryly.

"*Shh.*"

The two women take cotton balls and dip them into a liquid from one of Ms. Bea's bottles, and they begin to wipe their skin, removing their makeup layer by layer. The stuff must be strong, because Mrs. Smith keeps scrunching up her nose as if it smells bad. I wish we could hear what they are saying . . .

"Oh. My—"

"What?" I whisper. I stretch up on my tiptoes and squint through the glass and have to cover my mouth to keep from shrieking.

Whatever makeup remover the ladies are using has done its job: it's removed every single layer of makeup on their faces, and now they're rubbing it across their bare arms. What's revealed are thousands of tiny scars in the shape of stitches, which cover *every inch* of their skin. The plastic sheen is gone, leaving them looking faded and worn, like two rag dolls that were ripped apart and sewn back together.

I start to lose my grip on the windowsill. They're talking and smiling and laughing as if they're having a tea party. When the final scars are revealed, Ms. Bea reaches back into the case and pulls out a tube of some thick gunk that looks like putty or grout, something you'd buy at the hardware store, not a beauty shop. They each take a spatula-looking thing and start slathering the putty onto each other's faces, layer after layer after layer. It reminds me of that time Mrs. Anderson taught us how to make clay sculptures in art class: we used metal tools to shape the clay, scraping and pulling the mud in different directions. The sculptures were supposed to be self-portraits, but in the end my creation looked more like a monster than a reflection.

"Are you *seeing* this?" Mike whispers.

I blink in response, unable to form the words to express how I feel.

After a flawless coat of putty is applied, the women spray on a gloss coating that makes their skin look shiny and smooth once again, without a single scar showing. They sit back and smile at each other, admiring their handiwork. Ms. Bea smooths out her dress and begins to stand.

Mike tugs on my arm. "We need to go," he says, and together we dart across the street toward my house.

I unlock the door, and Mike barrels in first, practically knocking over my mom.

"Michael!"

"Sorry, Mrs. Parker," Mike says, bending over to catch his breath. "We were, umm, we were racing."

Mom raises an eyebrow. "In this heat? Come in the kitchen and get a drink before you both faint on me. And why are you all scratched up?"

"We took a shortcut," Mike says. "Through a thornbush."

Mom sighs. "Kitchen. Now. We've got Band-Aids and some water. And Grandma Jane left a batch of cookies."

We follow Mom to the kitchen, where she hooks us up with some first aid, water, and a plate of Grandma Jane's salted chocolate chip cookies. Neither of us speak. I think we're still in shock.

Mike leans toward me as Mom turns her back to make a cup of coffee.

"What. Was. That?" he whispers. Cookie crumbs spill from his mouth and he doesn't even seem to notice. "Why are they? They were so . . ."

"Scarred? I don't know."

"Do they all look like that? Marshall and the Browns, and Mrs. and Dr. Smith?"

"What about Dr. Smith?" Mom asks, turning around.

Mike's eyes widen. "Umm. Nothing."

I take in Mom's scrubs and suddenly put two and two together. "Hey, Mom, do you ever see him at the hospital?"

She nods. "Dr. Smith? Of course. He's a surgeon. Well, he *was*," she corrects herself. "He's been retired for who knows how long. He still shows up to volunteer, you know, just consulting with other doctors. But he doesn't work with the patients anymore."

Mike perks up beside me. "Do you know when he stopped practicing?"

Mom takes a deep sip from her mug as she leans against the counter. "I'm not sure," she says. "Must have been a while. He's been retired since I've been there." She shrugs and makes her way to the back door. "I'm going to enjoy my coffee on the deck," she says. "If you kids need anything, give me a yell. Come on, Billy."

Mike and I watch her and Billy disappear before exhaling.

"You owe me a month's worth of milkshakes," Mike says. "I like chocolate peanut butter and extra whipped cream."

"No way."

"That proves it, Parker. Your mom just told us the missing piece: Smith is a *surgeon*. He must be operating on the other Oldies."

"Yeah, he is," I tell him. "With dead body parts. Like Frankenstein."

"No, not like Frankenstein," he says. "Like a transplant. I googled it. Transplanting limbs is a legitimate thing. Dr. Smith is just doing it illegally."

"That can't be the whole story," I insist. "They've been around too long. There has to be some kind of magic they're using that has been keeping them alive for over a hundred years."

"That's a reach, Parker."

"We need to reach," I tell him. "Because something big is happening! I'm sure of it."

Mike opens his mouth to argue, but a knock on the front door stops him. Neither of us move. The knock comes again, and again, sounding so loud and forceful that I feel each one in my chest.

"Can't you hear the door, Quinn?" Mom asks, coming back through the kitchen. "I guess I'll get it."

A moment later, we hear the latch click and the hinges squeak.

"Mr. Marshall," Mom says. "What a nice surprise."

I freeze in my chair as Mike drops his cookie onto the table.

"I'm sorry to trouble you," Mr. Marshall says politely. "But I was wondering if your daughter and Michael Warren might be home?"

Instinctively I shake my head, even though Mom can't see me. *Say no, say no, Mom. Say no...*

"Sure. They're just having a snack," she answers. "Why? Is something wrong?"

"No, nothing like that," Mr. Marshall says. "It's just that I was hoping they could help me with a little weeding in my garden. My arthritis is acting up again. I'm happy to pay them for their trouble."

"Don't be silly. They'd love to help."

I'm still shaking my head as Mom calls us from the kitchen. "Quinn! Mike! Come here, please."

For a moment, Mike and I don't move, we just stare at each other. But Mom doesn't give up that easily.

"Hurry up, kids! Mr. Marshall doesn't have all day."

"Actually, it's Red," Mr. Marshall corrects her. "I prefer to go by my nickname. *Red.*" He repeats it loudly, and as the word hits my ears, I gasp.

"*Trust Red!*" I whisper to Mike. "It's the clue from my dad's casebook!"

"But what if it's a trick?" Mike asks.

"There's only one way to find out." I make my way to the door with Mike following at my heels.

Mr. Marshall—Red—is standing in the doorway, wearing

his dirt-stained gardening clothes with an old pair of work boots. Unlike the other Oldies, his skin is so wrinkled that it looks like tree bark. But when he smiles, it looks genuine: I can see the twinkle in his blue eyes.

"Hello, Quinn," he says.

"Hi, Red."

"See?" Mom says, patting me on the back. "The kids would love to help you. Just be sure to take water breaks if it gets too hot."

"I won't keep them long," Red promises. "Thank you, Mrs. Parker."

Mom waves goodbye as Mike and I follow Red across Goodie Lane. My stomach is flip-flopping all over the place as we step onto the side of the street with the colorful row of the Oldies' houses. Except, for the first time, I'm starting to realize that Red might not be an Oldie.

We stop in front of his tomato plants, which look perfectly weeded already. Red hands us each a pair of gardening gloves and he points to the plants.

"You might get your knees a little dirty, but you have to get close to the roots." He kneels down, and Mike and I follow suit.

"Pretend to pull up weeds," he instructs, his voice barely above a whisper. "They're probably watching."

"Who's *they*?" Mike asks, even though I know he knows the answer.

"The Oldies," Red says. Hearing that word coming out of his mouth sends a jolt through my limbs. "Don't worry," he adds quickly. "I may be old, but I'm not one of them. Keep weeding."

Mike and I exchange looks before we pretend to pull at leaves and stray blades of grass.

"Be careful. You don't want to pull out my plants."

"But there's nothing else to pull!"

"Just fake it. Like this—"

"What do you want?" I interrupt, staring hard into Red's eyes. "What do you know?"

"Too much," Red answers. "But I can't tell you here. Meet me at the library in an hour. I'll tell you everything then."

Mike evaluates Red, trying to decide whether or not he's telling the truth. "How do we know you're not messing with us?" he asks. "How do we know this isn't a trap?"

"You'll just have to trust me, I'm afraid."

"You have to be kidding—"

"We'll be there," I say, cutting Mike off before he can finish his sentence. "In the last study room all the way in the back. One hour."

Red nods. "One hour."

With this, I stand up, dust off my knees, and walk back across the street, with Mike following close behind.

"Are you sure about this, Parker?" he asks on my front stoop.

I take a breath and nod. "I'm sure. You want to come back in?"

"Nah," he says. "I need to go clean my room before my mom sees what a mess it is. I'll meet you outside in a little less than an hour."

"Cool. See you."

"See you, Parker. And I hope you're right about this guy."

I smile at him. "Am I ever wrong?"

He laughs loudly as he walks away.

The hour goes by painfully slowly. I sit outside with Mom and chat about school, eat about five more cookies, and go upstairs to reread Dad's notes again and again. When the clock finally shows me the number I've been waiting for, I grab my backpack, and yell goodbye to Mom. Mike is already outside, and together we zigzag along the sidewalk, past the Oldies' houses, which at the moment appear quiet and unsuspecting, before turning onto Main Street, as Mike claims it's the least-suspicious route. Here we dodge mailboxes and pedestrians, the sun beating down on us. We're both sweaty and ready for some air-conditioning by the time we reach the library.

"Come on," I say, racing Mike up the front steps.

We make our way inside and feel a rush of the blissful cold air.

"Is he here?" I ask, looking around.

"Don't think so. Let's check the room."

We follow the stairs down into the library's basement, which houses all of the study rooms. We quickly duck into the one where we met on our first research day: Red isn't inside yet. Mike and I get settled in our chairs, and within seconds there is a faint knock on the door.

"Come in," Mike calls.

The door slowly opens. In steps Red. "Hello," he says quietly.

"Hi," we say back.

There is an awkward moment when he stands there looking at us, and we sit there looking at him. Mike finally tells him to sit down. Red takes a seat in the corner and folds his hands in his lap.

"Thank you for meeting me here," he says. "I thought we could swap stories. Maybe figure out a way to help each other."

"How long have you known about the Oldies?" I ask.

His body stiffens at their name. "I've known them my whole life. I suppose that's why other people think I'm one of them."

"Were you guys friends?" Mike asks.

"No one has ever been friends with them aside from their little crew," Red explains. "My parents tried, but to no success. My grandmother used to say that they got mad when she refused to sell Bea the house after my grandfather died. I don't know why. They never seemed to care when someone moved in across the street, like you two." He nods to Mike and me. "Well, so long as you stay out of their way."

"Why has nobody wondered about their age?" I ask. "I mean, it just doesn't make sense."

"Oh, don't kid yourself, dear," he says. "The whole town *knows* something is off about them. But what questions could you ask to get truthful answers? And who wants to be the one to ask? Most people just keep to themselves, mind their own business. Besides, it doesn't hurt that they pump a constant stream of money into the town. Over the years they've donated God knows how much money to teams, schools, restaurants, the police station . . ."

"Did you know my dad?" I ask, my hands tingling. "I mean, I know you *knew* him, but did you ever talk to him about the others?"

Red purses his lips in a wave of sympathy. "Yes, dear. Your father was a good man. I feel for you and your mother about his loss. I, unfortunately, know all too well what it's like to lose someone you love."

I feel a sharp pain in my stomach now, as I do every time I talk about my dad. "How well did you know him? Did you see him a lot?"

"Your father first came to me about two years ago. That's when he found out about me and Mary."

"Mary *Hove*?"

"The one and only. You see, Mary and I lived across the street from each other. She grew up in your house, Quinn."

"I know."

He nods. "Yes, well, we went to high school together and worked on the school paper. I used to walk her home. We went to the movies every so often."

"Was Mary Hove your girlfriend?" Mike asks, his eyes bright.

Red smiles. "We never called it that, or made it to that point, but I can admit now that, yes, I would have liked her to be my girlfriend. I was quite fond of her. Back in those days, though, we took things much slower."

"What does Mary Hove have to do with the Oldies?"

"I'm not entirely sure," Red admits, shifting in his seat. "I can't help but think that they had something to do with her death. I was with Mary at the fireworks. We walked down to the beach together, I bought her an ice cream, we watched the show, and together we walked back to Goodie Lane. She even let me hold her hand."

Mike and I are breathless, leaning forward, listening with our whole bodies. "And then?"

"We said good night. I walked to my house, and from what I saw, she started to walk to her house—it was just across the street. But her parents say she never made it home." He takes a deep breath and pauses. I notice that his knuckles are white as he squeezes his hands together in his lap.

"Was she acting weird that week?"

"She said there was something about the pond," he continues slowly. "Something strange. During the last few weeks before Mary's death, she said that the pond was *calling* to her. She mentioned an orange light glowing at the bottom. And one night, I caught her standing at the edge, staring down in a trance. It was like she lost control of her own body. It scared me."

My stomach drops as I remember feeling pulled toward those same waters.

"Do you think the Oldies killed her?" I ask.

"I can't prove anything. Leading up to her death, Mary had been snooping around. She never told me what she found, but she told me she was suspicious of our neighbors, claiming that they were something supernatural. I regret not taking her more seriously."

At this I whack Mike in the arm. "See? I told you! Supernatural."

Mike pretends to look wounded as he rubs his shoulder. He turns to Red. "But couldn't the answer be surgical?" he asks. "I mean, how do we know that Smith isn't performing some kind of experimental limb transplants on the other Oldies? That would explain a lot, wouldn't it? The scars, the makeup, the new limbs . . ."

"*Frankensteins*," I whisper.

"Surgeon," Mike counters.

Red simply shrugs his bony shoulders. "I wish I had more answers. I honestly don't know what their secret is, only that they have a big one."

I shake my head in disbelief. "Wait, hold on. You've been onto them for *decades*, right?"

Red nods.

"Why didn't you *say* anything? Why didn't you go to the police?"

"I *did* go to the police!" Red looks away with frustration. "Twice. The first time was right after Mary's death. I was laughed out of the station. I didn't go back for years. Mary was always the brave one. I was better at the behind-the-scenes stuff. The research."

"But you did go back?" Mike asks. "To the police?"

"Eventually, yes. The second time was when my wife was still alive. The officer on duty filed a report, but I think it was just to humor me. I don't think he believed a word of it." Red exhales, deflated. "When I got home, I had a card waiting for me. It was very under the radar, but to me the message was clear."

"What message?" I ask.

"That for the sake of my kids, I needed to stop poking my nose where it didn't belong." He runs a hand over his face. "I was scared, so I pulled back. It wasn't until your dad got involved that I started tracking them again. My wife was gone, my kids had moved away with families of their own. I figured I had nothing to lose."

"I think Mr. Brown has my dad's leg," I suddenly blurt out.

"Unfortunately, I think you're right," Red says. "From what I can tell, our neighbors seem to pick and choose their bits and pieces when the bodies come into the Phoenix. Then, from what I can tell, they sew the parts on themselves somehow, and seal the deal in the pond."

"*Seal the deal in the pond?*" I repeat in disbelief. "What do you mean?"

"I don't exactly know. What I do know is that once I caught them swimming in it at midnight. When they came out, their bodies were sort of glowing. They seemed rejuvenated. I don't know how else to describe it."

"That doesn't prove anything," Mike argues. "Maybe they just like skinny-dipping."

"*Mike,*" I scold.

Red makes a face. "I've only seen them do it once, and they wore white robes." He looks at Mike. "So no, son, no skinny-dipping."

"Did you see a light in the pond?" I ask.

"Never. Your father never did either, at least not that he told me." He frowns. "Why do you ask?"

My body stiffens. "I saw the light," I admit. "And . . ."

Red leans forward. "And what, Quinn?"

"And a face. A woman with dark hair was calling my name from the water."

It feels strange to say the words out loud. Mike's eyes widen.

"You didn't tell me that!"

"Yes, I did."

"I think I would have remembered you seeing a woman in the pond, Parker."

"It's not my fault you never listen to me."

Red holds up two hands, silencing us. He then takes a long, slow exhale, as if collecting his thoughts. "Quinn." The seriousness with which he says my name causes me to shiver. "You have to stay away from the pond. It's dangerous."

"But what if it's a clue? What if the pond is the key to unlock the mystery?" My pulse is racing. "What if it's Mary trying to tell me something?"

"It's not Mary. It's a trick. Don't you get it? They're onto you."

"Whatever, we're not scared of them," Mike says, his voice slightly higher than normal.

"You should be," Red says. "And I'm here to help you. But we have to be safe about this. I'm not about to sit by and watch you get hurt like Mary."

We all exchange looks. My leg starts to bounce and I

have to press both hands against my knee to stop it. This entire situation has gotten too real. The investigation is no longer a way to pass the time and remember my dad: it's life or death. And we need a plan.

"So," I say. "What next? What do we do?"

"I think we should meet here again on Saturday," Red says, "with the goal of tracking the Oldies' every move from now until the fireworks."

"Why the fireworks?"

Red lowers his gaze. "That's the anniversary of her ... of Mary's ..."

Her death. Or worse: her *murder.*

"That makes sense," I tell him. "Mike and I will finish school this week, so we'll have more time to spy."

Mike drums his fingers against the desk. "This feels like the kind of thing that should have a secret code name."

Red gives a small, amused smile. "What did you have in mind?"

"What about *Hove*?" I suggest.

Mike shakes his head. "Too obvious. What about *Ghost Hunter*?" He looks at me. "You know, for your dad."

A warmth rushes over me at his words. Red nods.

"Operation Ghost Hunter it is."

CHAPTER 12

Saturday feels forever away. I try to throw myself into the end-of-school activities with some enthusiasm, but it's near impossible for me to care about yearbook signings and indoor field days when I'm sure that something sinister is going on so close to home.

My friends, for their part, are nothing but excited.

"I'm *so* glad we're here at Rocky Hill," Lex gushes at lunch. "Bedford just has a normal last week for their seventh graders, and I hear that their teachers are still giving homework."

"They must be dying," Zoe mumbles, picking apart her sandwich. She turns to me. "You're definitely coming tonight, right?" she asks me with a wary look. "You're not going to ditch me again and make up some excuse about your nonexistent science homework?"

I shift uncomfortably in my seat. The school dance was Lex's idea: she's on the school spirit committee and came up with the Come as Your Favorite Holiday theme. Mike and I are supposed to meet tonight to make a plan for Saturday, but I can't blow off Zoe again. For one thing, I'm all out of lies, and for another, I miss her.

"Of course I'm coming," I say, trying my best to sound excited.

"What are you two dressing up as?" Kaylee asks.

"Witches," Zoe and I say in unison. For the first time in weeks, Zoe flashes me a big smile.

Lex nods approvingly. "Halloween? Solid choice."

I smile at Zoe across the table, and together we discuss our costumes, our black dresses and pointy hats, and the time that Zoe's mom will pick me up for the dance. I feel Mike watching me across the way as we talk, and I do my best to ignore him, but he's persistent. And after lunch, he follows me to my locker.

"Are we on for tonight? Operation Ghost Hunter?" His eyes are bright and excited.

I shrink back against my locker. "I can't."

At this, his brows furrow. "What are you talking about? Why not?"

I shift in my sneakers, stuffing my hands into my pockets. "I'm going to the dance."

Mike stares at me for a beat, his face in disbelief. "Are you kidding?"

"It's just one night."

"But every night can make a difference," he says, the annoyance creeping into his voice. "We barely have any time left until the Fourth of July. We have to figure out the Oldies before then. What if they're planning another murder?"

"I know," I mumble. "I just feel like I need this tonight. This investigation has taken over my whole life the last few weeks. I miss my friends."

Mike shakes his head. "Didn't you say that we had to see this through?"

"I'm sorry," I say softly. "I just can't let my best friend down again."

He rubs his temples with his fingers, staring at the ground. "Fine," he says. "Fine, go to the dance. I'll just catch up with you tomorrow."

He walks away before I can even answer him. The guilt sinks in once I'm alone, but there's no going back now. I promised Zoe. I can't lie to her again.

Mike doesn't wait for me after school. He doesn't reply to my *I'm sorry* text. He doesn't even wave when we see each other walking home.

Up in my bedroom, I pull out my witch costume,

assembling the pieces bit by bit: my black dress, my black high-tops, and dark eyeliner around my eyes.

A horn blares from the street.

"Bye, Billy," I call as I grab my hat and trot out to Zoe's mom's car.

"You look awesome!" Zoe exclaims.

"That's because I look just like you," I say.

We laugh as her mom pulls out of the driveway, and for the first time in weeks, I don't bother to look toward the Oldies' houses.

When we get to school, Lex and Kaylee are waiting for us at the front of the gym. Lex is fully decked out in shades of pink and red to represent Valentine's Day, and Kaylee is dressed like a cute little rodent for Groundhog Day. The gym itself looks like the teachers donated all of their holiday decor. Nothing goes with anything, but it *is* kind of festive.

The music is already blaring: heavy bass, catchy lyrics. A small group of confident girls start squealing and race toward the DJ station to dance. A slew of shyer kids hover along the edges of the gym, hands stuffed in pockets, trying to look cool, with only a few brave souls daring to jump into the mix.

Without warning, Lex grabs my hand and drags me toward the center of the action. She flails her body around, belting out the lyrics at the top of her lungs. I can't help but laugh and sing along. Zoe and Kaylee are soon at our sides, bopping along with the rest of us. My body is completely relaxed.

But then the DJ has to go and play a slow song.

Half of the kids immediately filter out while a new flock filters in, suddenly brave enough to wrap their arms around a classmate and sway.

Zoe looks at me. "Want to go get some juice?"

I nod, realizing how sweaty I am. She leads me toward the refreshment table and hands me a Dixie cup of room-temperature apple juice.

I thank her and chug it.

"I'll go grab us some more," Zoe says, turning back around for seconds.

As soon as she steps away, someone taps me on the shoulder.

"Jeez, Parker, save some for the rest of us," Mike says. He's dressed as what I assume is a pathetic Christmas tree, with half-broken twigs duct-taped to his green T-shirt.

"What are you doing here?" I ask, not bothering to hide my shock.

He smiles somewhat shyly, scratching the back of his head. "I felt kind of bad," he says softly. "I mean, what's the harm in one night off from the case?"

I nod, and we stand in silence for an awkward second or two.

"Sweet costume," I finally say, my tone full of sarcasm. "You really went all out, huh? And the Yankees hat just screams *holiday*."

"You're just jealous," he says with a smirk.

"Umm," Zoe says, cutting in between us. "What's going on with you two? You're acting all weird again. I mean, are you together or *not*?"

"Together," Mike says quickly. "Very much together."

"Then what are you standing around for? Go dance!"

"With *him*?" I balk.

Zoe rolls her eyes. "No, with our math teacher. Of course with him. Go!"

Before I can answer, Zoe reaches over and snatches away my empty cup, waving us toward the dance floor. Mike shrugs and takes my hand, leading me into the crowd of couples. I'm not breathing—*breathe, Quinn!* I exhale loudly. Too loudly. Mike wraps his arms around my waist and I become very aware of the fact that I am still very sweaty. I try to pull back a little and end up bopping him in the head with the brim of my witch hat.

"Wow, Parker. I guess you're a better runner than dancer, huh?"

"Ha ha."

"Just kidding. Relax." He pulls me in a bit closer and I'm afraid I might faint. Not because of Mike but because of the *heat*. He's too close, there's no air, there are too many couples around us stealing our space and our oxygen. I can feel Lex staring at us from my immediate left. *It's no big deal*, I want to shout. But then again, it kind of *is* a big deal. I'm here dancing with my neighbor, my friend, Mike Warren, someone who has annoyed me forever. Except right now he doesn't feel like just a friend, and in this moment, I'm so not annoyed.

I allow my arms to loosen their grip around his neck and my hips to sway more gently in time with the music. Just when I finally start to relax, the song ends. He pulls away before I do, and my arms fall before I'm ready to let go.

"I'm going to go get a drink," he says abruptly. Before I can offer to join him, he walks away, not even glancing back in my direction.

Zoe is already at my side. "What happened?" she cries over the music. "Why'd he run off like that?"

"I don't even know," I sigh. "Can we just dance?"

I don't have to ask a second time: Zoe is all over the dance floor, and soon enough, Lex and Kaylee join us. For a moment, I forget about Mike, and I pretend not to notice or care when he stares me down from the sidelines in a huddle of boys as I continue to dance with my friends.

"You OK?" Zoe whispers in between songs. I nod stiffly, and out of the corner of my eye, I watch Mike make his way toward the exit.

"Never better," I lie, tossing my head back toward the gym lights.

The next morning, I wake up with a wicked case of bed head and humiliation. I shouldn't have danced with Mike last night. I shouldn't have allowed myself to be swept up in the moment. I mean, who does he think he is, anyway? He's so full of himself, and really, not even *that* cute. The fake romance needs to end: I need to initiate a fake breakup. From this point forward, Mike and I are strictly partners, and once we crack the Oldies case, we're *nothing*. We're done. We're just two people who happen to live next door to each other.

Mom smiles and snaps a series of pictures of me on her phone when I come down the stairs.

"What are you doing?" I cry, covering my face.

"Happy last day of school!" She hands me a cupcake and snaps another picture. "I can't believe my baby is going to be an eighth grader. One more year and you'll be in *high school*! Then college. Then . . ." Another picture.

"Calm down, Mom. It's just the end-of-the-year concert. No big deal." But I take the cupcake all the same. "Did you bake this yourself?"

"No such luck. But I should still get points for getting up extra early to get to the grocery store this morning. They were just putting them out."

"You never let me have sugar in the morning."

She sits down across from me at the kitchen table. "Today is special."

I take a large bite out of the cupcake. Mom did good. She got my favorite. Lemon coconut. I smile and give her a thumbs-up. Mom beams back at me.

"Are you excited?" she asks. "Nervous? Sad?"

"None of the above," I say honestly. "It's not even a big deal. It's not like I'm graduating."

"Then why do you look so fired up? Like a girl on a mission."

I shove another large bite of cupcake into my mouth. *If she only knew . . .*

Mom suddenly slaps the table as she notices the time. "Oh, we have to move, honey. Hurry up. You have to get dressed! We can't be late for the concert. And I want a good seat."

I let her hustle me back upstairs. My dress is already laid out. Mom and I bought it together a month ago from the new store in the mall. It's green, sleeveless, and has eyelet details around the neck. I slip it on and let Mom snap another slew of pictures, oohing and ahhing and practically crying in the process.

"I wish your father could see you now," she says, swiping at a tear.

My whole body aches with the comment and all I can do

is nod silently in response. Mom comes over and squeezes me, and I can't hold it in anymore. I'm crying in her arms. I'm picturing all of the photographs today that he won't be in, the empty seat in the audience where he should be sitting. It isn't fair. It's just a stupid concert, but it's still not fair. Billy moans at our feet, as though he is crying along with us.

"It's OK, baby," Mom whispers into my hair. "You're allowed to miss him. I miss him, too." She strokes my wet cheek. Suddenly she pulls back and rubs my shoulders. "Tell you what, we'll photoshop his face into one of the pictures. That way he'll be there in spirit and there in the photo album."

I swipe at my tears. "Do you even know how to photoshop? You're, like, *really* bad with computers."

Mom ruffles my hair. "Hey, I'm getting better. I can always have your aunt help us. She's good at that stuff." She squeezes my arms again and looks at the clock on the wall. "I think it's time to go. You ready?"

I take a deep breath and nod. "Let's do it."

We climb into the car, and I rest my head against the window as Mom pulls out onto Goodie Lane. My eyes automatically shift toward the end of the cul-de-sac, toward the pond. I have the sudden urge to go to the water, to lean over the edge and stare down into the darkness until a face appears. The urge is so strong that before I know it, my fingers are gripping the door handle, only letting go after Mom swings the car onto Main Street and away from Goodie Lane; the turn is too sharp, and it jolts me in my seat.

"Whoopsie," she says.

My heart thumps faster in my chest and I drop my hand back onto my lap. I think about Red and what he said about staying away from the pond, but what if he's wrong? What if it really *is* Mary Hove, trying to give me a clue from the other side?

"Oh, I love this one," Mom interrupts, turning up the radio. It's playing the song that Mike and I danced to last night. I pound the power button with my thumb, turning it off, and Mom looks sideways at me.

"What was that about?"

"Nothing. I'm just sick of that song."

"*Right* . . ." She looks suspicious but doesn't push it as she parks. "Let's just get you inside." She snaps another picture of me walking into the building. I threaten to take her phone away. Mom leans over and kisses me on the cheek. "I'm going to go save a seat for your grandma Jane. Good luck, honey!"

She scurries off toward the auditorium, and I make my way to the music room where the seventh graders are being held until the concert. Zoe waves me down as soon as I walk in.

"I *love* your dress!" she squeals. "How have I not borrowed that before?"

"It's new," I reply, smiling. My body relaxes as we compare outfits until Lex and Kaylee approach, but it immediately stiffens again as Mike walks in the room.

Zoe squeezes my arm. "What the heck is going on with you two? One minute you can't stop staring at each other, and the next you're not speaking."

"It's complicated," I mutter.

Zoe nudges me in the arm and smiles. "Come on, don't let him ruin your day. Besides, I've got your back. Say the word and I'll go over there—"

"It's OK," I interrupt. "I've got it."

I take a deep breath as he approaches. *He doesn't really like you. And you don't really like him. You need to focus on the case. Just keep things professional . . .*

"Hey, Parker."

"Hey." I smile coolly.

Mike raises his eyebrows and leans in close to me. "I have to talk to you."

"Kind of busy right now." I gesture to Zoe for emphasis.

"It'll just take a second."

"Can't you hear?" Zoe interrupts, standing between us. "She's *busy*."

"It's important—"

"Roll call!" Mrs. Boulton announces loudly from the front of the room. "Come, come. We need you all to line up alphabetically. Let's get this show on the road."

I smile at Mike, break away from the group, and join the middle of the line. He works his way to the other end, and I feel a sting of regret as I meet his eyes, wishing that I knew what he wanted to talk about.

Zoe, meanwhile, gives me a thumbs-up from the *J* section, where she stands in front of Marion Jones. I smile weakly at her as Mrs. Boulton barks out instructions on how to walk slowly and gracefully to the auditorium stage. She presents a last-minute list of dos and don'ts before the band teacher strikes up the ensemble and the procession begins. One by one we walk forward as we've been taught: left foot, pause, right foot, pause, and so on. My mom and Grandma Jane stand up and start howling as soon as they spot me. I laugh and wave in spite of Mrs. Boulton's instructions to "stay in the zone." Mom snaps pictures as Grandma Jane struggles to balance her digital camera. The majority of parents in the audience are standing up and taking pictures, hollering words of praise at their kids, and waving balloons. Pointless or not, it's actually quite festive and I start to feel pumped up the same way I do before a big track meet.

There's just one thing missing: Dad. It's hard seeing the other dads in the audience, even the ones who are staring at their phones, looking like they would rather be anywhere but here. I guess I can't really blame them for being bored, but I know that if my dad were here, he'd be whooping and hollering with the best of them. I remember the last track meet he came to and the way that he yelled at the top of his lungs as he jumped up and down on the bleachers. His face was beet red and he had the biggest smile. After the meet, he took Mom, Grandma Jane, and me to Harvey's, where we ordered supersized milkshakes. Extra sprinkles.

"Please rise for the national anthem," Mrs. Boulton says, interrupting my thoughts.

The audience stands, and a kid from my Language Arts class takes the mic to belt out the song. We then collectively say the Pledge of Allegiance, before launching into a cheesy class version of "Stand by Me." When the song is finished and the audience's cheering dies down, Mrs. Boulton leads us into our next series of numbers, alternating between solos and group songs. The finale has us singing and walking out into the audience, weaving in and out of the rows and around the back where the overflow of families stands. The plan is for us to end up singing next to our relatives, but Mrs. Boulton gave strict instructions for us to stay in line and in order until the last bar. I follow closely behind Janae Park as we snake around chairs, laughing and singing, riding the high that is the last day of school.

Until I hear it . . .

"Par-ker, Par-ker, Par-ker..."

Slowly, I turn to the right. *It can't be.*

"Par-ker, Par-ker, Par-ker..."

The slow clap starts just like at the track meet. I hear it loud and clear over the rest of the cheering and the music. My eyes track the sound, and sure enough, there they are, the Oldies, lined up across the back corner of the room, chanting my name. I want to turn and run the other way but I can't. The procession pushes me forward. Soon enough I am right in front of them: Bea, Attwood, the Browns, and the Smiths. Each one is holding a white balloon. I stiffen and try my best to look unfazed in their presence, but it's near impossible with their rubber smiles and soulless eyes bearing down on me. They each take a step toward me.

Is anyone else seeing this? I swing my head to the left and right, but everyone else is cheering and dancing and completely absorbed in their own celebrations.

Suddenly I feel a sharp hand on my shoulder. Ms. Bea's claw-like fingers dig fiercely into the skin with shocking strength. She continues to smile as she hisses in my ear, "We're watching you, pretty girl."

I rip my arm away and break free from my spot in line, bolting toward my mom and Grandma Jane. Mrs. Boulton beckons wildly for me to get back in line, but my lead has caused everyone else to also run toward their loved ones. Mom embraces me tightly and I just want to cry from her warmth and safety. She and Grandma Jane huddle around me, taking pictures, hugging me, congratulating me. The volume in the auditorium has magnified since the procession was broken: happy families, happy students ready for summer and the beginning of something bigger. Despite all of the noise, I can still hear the sinister chant behind me: *"Par-ker, Par-ker, Par-ker . . ."*

I peer through my mother's arms, but the Oldies have disappeared. In their place, the six white balloons float up to the rafters like ghosts.

CHAPTER 13

I can't sleep. Every time I close my eyes, I see the white balloons hovering over my bed and hear the Oldies' laughter piercing through the night.

"Whoa," Mom says to me in the morning, lifting my chin to inspect my tired face. "You look like you had a rough night."

"Kind of," I admit.

"Why didn't you come get me?" Her face softens. "Was it because of yesterday? Because your dad wasn't there?"

I freeze, and Mom interprets my silence as a sign, and she squeezes me hard against her chest.

"You going to be OK while I'm at work?"

I pull back and notice her scrubs for the first time. "Yeah, I'm fine."

"Take it easy, OK?" she instructs. "Relax. No running. Just have a cozy couch day. When I come home, we'll order pizza."

"Sounds good."

She kisses my forehead before heading for the door. "See you later, honey. Text me if you need me." Mom then opens the front door, and shrieks. "Oh, Michael! You startled me!"

My stomach tightens. *Mike?*

"Morning, Mrs. Parker."

"This is becoming a habit."

"Yeah, I'm sorry. I just needed to talk to Quinn. Is she home?"

"It's cool, Mom," I tell her. "I'll see you after work." I step out onto the front steps beside Mike, but I refuse to meet his eyes. Together we wave goodbye to my mom as she pulls out of the driveway. When her car is out of sight, Mike turns to me.

"I need to talk to you," he says.

"You can't keep doing this," I tell him.

"Doing what?"

"*This.* Just dropping by whenever you feel like it." I frown at him. "It's annoying."

Mike blinks, looking a bit wounded by my words. "What's your problem, Parker?"

"I don't have a problem." I stare at the Oldies' houses and remember the white balloons. I exhale deeply. It's not Mike's fault. I know that. So why am I being so rude to him?

"Whatever, Parker," Mike says. "We don't have time to fight about nothing. We've got a mission, remember?"

"How can I forget?"

"Then get dressed! We've got one hour to get to the Phoenix before it opens."

My bones freeze. "The Phoenix?"

Mike nods. "I'll explain on the way. You with me?"

I give a hesitant nod back.

"And wear your running gear. We have to make it look like we're just on a normal run, nothing suspicious."

He turns to go down the stoop but suddenly stops and faces me again. "By the way, I liked dancing with you," he tells me. "I guess I just got, I don't know . . . Nervous." Before I can answer, he hops down the steps and is gone, leaving me to melt on my own doorstep.

Thirty minutes later, we meet outside. Mike is wearing his favorite running shoes and a game face.

"You ready?"

"As I'll ever be."

Just like normal, we stretch with Billy watching us from the living room window. I follow Mike out onto the driveway, and my feet feel heavier than usual, as if there are weights tied to my ankles.

Across the street, Bea leads the other Oldies in their morning watering ritual, their roses in such a perfect state of bloom that I can smell them from my house. I don't have to look up to feel their cold eyes watching us. Red, on the other hand, tends to his tomato plants as if he hasn't a care in the world.

"What's the plan?" I whisper to Mike.

"The Browns don't open the funeral home until nine. That gives us an hour to get over there and back."

"Get there and back to do *what*?"

"Take a look around. See if anything is out of the ordinary."

My stomach turns. "I don't think I can do that."

"I wouldn't ask you if I thought we had another option, Parker," he says. "But we're running out of time."

Without waiting for an answer, he takes off down the street, leaving me with no choice but to run after him. The Oldies watch us as we go, with Red giving the subtlest of nods before we disappear onto Main Street, avoiding the pond as we fly.

"This is wild," I tell Mike. "How are we even going to get in?"

At this, he smiles and pulls out a set of keys from the pocket of his basketball shorts.

"Are those?"

"Yup."

I stop running and grip his arm, pulling us both to a dead halt. "How?"

"Red gave them to me. We have an hour to get them back. One hour to get in and out." His face turns pleading. "Come on, what do we have to lose?"

"Everything," I say, but I start running again just the same.

As we round toward the center of town, the large white building comes into view, the pillars reaching up toward the sun, the black shutters framing old windows with uneven bull's-eyes blown in the glass. A foreboding sign sits on the manicured lawn, reading *Phoenix Funeral Home*. Every inch of my body turns to ice, and I freeze just like last time. My heart seems to beat in my throat.

Mike gently takes my hand, which only makes my heart beat faster.

"Are you going to be OK?" he asks, his face full of concern. "I can do this part by myself—I'm sorry. I mean, it's important, but I don't want you to feel—"

"I'm fine," I lie, letting his hand drop. He's right: we don't have any other option. The Oldies are keeping secrets, and this is the best place to look. I grit my teeth and look straight ahead. "Which door?"

Mike studies me before ducking toward the back of the building. I follow him to a side entrance, half-hidden behind an overgrown rosebush. Mike fumbles with the keys for a second until he finds one that fits, letting us inside.

The smell is the first thing that hits me: the familiar stench of flowers, candles, and chemicals. Mike and I tip-toe down the narrow hallway, until we reach the lobby. The place looks the same as I remember it. The entranceway is a dull gray, lined with gold trim, muted area rugs, a collection of dusty books placed haphazardly on a side bookcase, and a worn couch with some throw pillows added to make the place appear homey. In front of us there are two narrow hallways, and I remember them both well: one leads to the Browns' office and conference room and the other leads to the memorial service rooms.

The last time I was here, I puked in one of the potted plants.

The last time I was here was when I said goodbye to my dad.

Mike is studying me. "You sure you're OK? You can go outside and play lookout instead if you want."

I think back to my dad's casebooks, pages upon pages of spy notes on the Oldies, codes that Mike and I have yet to figure out. I visualize Mr. Brown wearing my dad's leg, sprinting around the neighborhood and silently rubbing it in my face each time we cross paths. I think about the track meet. And the concert yesterday. And the number of times I had to cancel on my friends in order to investigate. No, I can't let them win.

"I'm staying," I tell Mike. "Come on."

I lead us down the left hallway toward the office. Mike set the alarm on his phone to beep every ten minutes so that we don't lose track of time. The plan is to inspect each room in no more than ten minutes, getting us out of the Phoenix and back on our run by the time the Oldies start to leave Goodie Lane.

I stare at my feet as we walk, desperate not to lose my nerve. The lights seem to dim as we turn a corner. The walls morph to a sickly white, and the smell of chemicals becomes more potent with each step toward the office. The door is unlocked, but we leave the lights off as we search, using the flashlights on our phones. The office itself is painted a dark eggplant color, making the space feel even tighter than it already is. Along the back wall is a row of locked filing cabinets and an empty desk.

"Where's the computer? Or the printer?" Mike whispers.

I shrug and move over to the framed artworks, hung crookedly on the wall in wooden frames. They look like inkblots, like someone spilled a pot of paint onto yellowed pieces of paper. It seems strange to hang something so ominous.

The alarm buzzes, startling us both. Mike and I exchange looks, disappointed that we haven't found a single clue yet.

"Let's try the memorial rooms," he suggests.

My stomach turns as we tiptoe back the way we came, around the twisty hallway with the creaky floorboards. We pass the potted plant that I had thrown up in last year, and I feel sick again just looking at it.

"You keep guard out here," Mike tells me. "I'll be quick."

I don't bother to argue. I stand with my back pressed up against the wall and my phone hugged tightly against my chest as I tick off the seconds in my head until Mike finally comes back.

"Nothing," he says.

This entire investigation is starting to feel like one big dead end.

Mike looks at me, his eyebrows raised. "Last place to check is the basement."

I agree despite how dizzy I feel. Even though this place is empty, it's hotter in here than it is outside.

After quickly checking the time, we circle back toward the lobby and the first set of hallways. We walk, swinging our flashlights on our phones back and forth, until we find one last door. It's painted white to blend in with the wall, and if it wasn't for the glint of the metal doorknob, we would have totally missed it.

"A hidden door? Well, that's not creepy at all," Mike jokes.

But I don't laugh. Something feels off.

"What do you think is down there?" I ask.

"Only one way to find out."

I take a deep, full breath as Mike turns the knob, and I follow him closely down the stairs until we reach a basement.

It's all concrete, bare white walls with a row of steel shelves lining two sides of the room, packed with glass jars and metal cans that I can't read the labels of. In the far corner, there are a bunch of clear tubes and large cylinders marked with the word POND. And against the back wall is a floor-to-ceiling unit of oversized drawers. A utility sink rests beside us by the staircase, and right in front is a flat table with a floor light positioned to its left.

"This must be where they prepare the bodies," Mike says, his voice shaking. "The drawers . . ." He points across the room. "Do you think there are *people* in those?"

I've never seen Mike Warren this afraid of anything, so even though my knees feel as though they might buckle beneath me, I take a deep breath and put on my bravest face.

"The clock is ticking," I say. "Let's look around."

We float through the room, hesitating in front of supplies that I don't recognize.

"I don't know what's normal for this place and not," I admit, taking in the tools lined up along a metal tray. It reminds me of the dentist's office, only these tools are larger and much more menacing. "How do we know if any of this stuff is illegal?"

"I don't know," Mike says.

We continue to look around until the strong, chemical smell starts to make me feel nauseous.

"Maybe we should just get out of here."

"Yeah, let's go."

We're about to move when a noise above causes us to freeze. Footsteps.

Mike's eyes widen. "Did you—"

"*Shh!*"

I take a step closer to Mike so that our arms are pressed against each other. We hold our breath and listen: someone's moving up there.

I snatch Mike's phone, looking helplessly at the timer, which shows that we still have seven minutes, not even counting the extra ten-minute cushion Mike had accounted for. "I thought you said no one would be here now?" I stop the clock: The alarm is pointless.

For once, Mike is speechless, his face stiff in horror.

Suddenly, the basement door opens. I grab Mike's hand and drag him behind the oversized cylinder. We crouch, listening to a series of heavy steps coming down the wooden stairs.

"You just get yourself comfy on the table," a man's voice says. "I'm going to wash my hands."

"Okeydokey!" a cheerful woman responds.

Mike and I peer around the side of the canister. Ms.

Attwood is sitting on the edge of the metal table in her floral yellow sundress, her legs swinging back and forth.

"Oh, I do love summer, don't you?" she asks.

"A bit hot for my taste," Dr. Smith says from the sink. He turns around and pulls on a pair of oversized black rubber gloves. "I don't remember it always being so humid in this town."

"Nonsense! It's been much hotter. Don't you remember the summer of '26? And then '52? At least now we have air-conditioning."

My jaw drops and I poke Mike in the ribs, shooting him an *I told you so* look. His entire face is frozen in horror.

"True," Dr. Smith says. "I wonder how we ever survived without it." He walks over to the drawers. "Just the arms today, right, Rose?"

"That's right."

Dr. Smith leans over one of the canisters marked POND and pulls out two human arms. "Angela picked out a good pair for you this time."

"Good. These ones have had it. They've already got the arthritis."

"They wear out so quickly these days, don't they," he says, placing the arms delicately onto the table beside Ms. Attwood. "Would you be a dear and remove your cardigan?"

"Oh, of course."

Ms. Attwood slips off her cardigan, and Dr. Smith leans

over and begins to draw a dotted line in black marker across the shoulders of both of her arms, just along where her sundress opens.

"We'll make you good as new," he says, before wiping down the skin with a brown liquid. He then picks up an electric saw.

I grip Mike's hand tighter and bite down hard on my lip. I want to close my eyes, but I can't. It's as if my lids are frozen open. I hear Mike's uneven breaths beside me, and we both jump as the electric saw roars to life, making hideous contact with Ms. Attwood's right shoulder.

I brace myself for blood, but there is none, not even a drop. Ms. Attwood, for her part, doesn't even flinch.

"How are things going at the Town Hall?" Dr. Smith asks casually, raising his voice to be heard over the growl of the saw.

"Oh, you know how it goes. It's a million times easier to update our records these days now that everything is digital. And no one's ever suspicious of little old me." She winks at Dr. Smith, who laughs alongside her.

"No nosy Nellies this year?"

"Nothing that a little money can't handle," Ms. Attwood says. Her eyes narrow. "Unless, of course, you count the cop's daughter across the street."

Every inch of my body turns to ice. Mike squeezes my hand harder. Painful tingles creep across my limbs. Dr.

Smith has finished sawing off the right arm and begins sawing off the left one without skipping a beat.

"Is she it then?" he asks. "The sacrifice on the Fourth of July?"

Ms. Attwood puckers her lips as if she just sipped on something sour. "I suppose. It's a shame, really. So young. But alas, it must be done if we want Beatrice's new spell to work. We must be fit and free."

"Fit and free indeed," Dr. Smith says.

He then pulls up a stool and begins sewing the new arms onto Ms. Attwood's old shoulders with thick black thread, just like a rag doll. When he's finished, he takes off his gloves and pats Ms. Attwood on the back. "There we have it," he says. "After your swim tonight, you'll be as good as new."

"I wish these upgrades lasted a little longer," Ms. Attwood says, a whiny tone to her voice. "Our bodies seem to get worn out much quicker these days."

"Beatrice is doing her best," Dr. Smith says. "Now, let me take a look at you." He steps back and examines Ms. Attwood's new limbs, which she shakes around in exaggerated circles with a childlike laugh. "Perfect," he says, and leads her to the staircase.

Ms. Attwood tugs her cardigan back on. "Should we lock up?" she asks, throwing one last look around the room.

"No need. Angela and Jon should be on their way. Do you want a lift to the Town Hall?"

"I think I'll walk," Ms. Attwood says, her heeled feet climbing the stairs as she talks. "Get some use out of these old legs before we swap them out."

Dr. Smith chuckles. I hold my breath until their voices disappear, the door upstairs slamming shut behind them.

Mike's eyes are still wide. He holds up five fingers and silently counts down. On *one* we both barrel up the stairs and down the white hallway, until we finally spill out of the side door. The thorns from the rosebush claw at our skin as we continue to run while half-blinded by the sun. On the sidewalk, we pass Ms. Attwood, who gives us a look as we jet around the corner. We continue running until we are standing in front of Harvey's, where Mike finally lets go of my sweaty hand.

"What are we doing here?" I ask, breathless.

"I owe you a milkshake," he pants, tugging me inside the cool, brightly lit shop. "A lot of milkshakes."

"Does this mean you believe me now?"

He sighs, defeated. "How can I not?"

Inside, a high school student escorts us to a colorful booth in the back, the pinks and greens and sweet-smelling room a welcome contrast to the Phoenix. Mike hands me a menu.

"I don't think I can stomach anything," I tell him.

"Me neither," he admits, folding the menus in front of us. "But we have to. I read that sugar helps to prevent our bodies from going into shock."

"Are we in shock?"

"I don't know." He pulls up the symptoms on his phone. "Are you dizzy?"

"Yes."

"Clammy?"

"I guess."

"Nauseous?"

"Very."

He shrugs and puts his phone down. "I'm not a doctor, but I think we should at least share a shake to be safe."

"Fine," I mutter. "But only if it's cookie dough."

The faintest of smiles crosses his lips. "Cookie dough it is." He flags down our waiter and puts in our order, and we both sit quietly as we wait for it to arrive in a large clear glass, piled high with whipped cream and chocolate chips. The waiter drops off two straws, two spoons, and a silver cup full of the extra milkshake.

"Enjoy," he tells us, before disappearing back into the kitchen.

Mike pushes the glass toward me. "You first."

I take a sip, and the sweetness is like a sucker punch to the gut. I push it back to him. He takes a sip and frowns.

"OK, now I'm mad," he says. "The Oldies have ruined my milkshake: This means war."

I don't care about the milkshake. My hands can't stop

shaking as I repeat one word in my head: *sacrifice*. I'm to be the *sacrifice*!

Mike eyes me from across the table. "You don't look too good, Parker. You really should take a sip of this."

"I don't want a sip." I can feel tears welling in my eyes. "Didn't you hear them? They said I'm going to be the sacrifice. On the Fourth!"

He chews on the end of the straw, thinking. "That's why we've got to stop them."

"But what *was* that?" I ask, my voice high and unsteady. "Did we just see what I think we saw? I mean, should we *tell* someone?"

"Red," Mike says quietly. "We can only tell Red. You said so yourself: no one else will believe us."

"But how was that possible?"

"Why are you so surprised, Parker? I thought you'd be happy. This proves your whole Frankenstein theory was right. You win." He lifts the glass, pretending to toast me with the milkshake.

I stiffen in the booth. "I don't want to *win*. I want to stop them."

"Then we need to be smart about this. We need to figure out what is keeping them alive. You saw Attwood. She didn't even feel the saw."

"And there was no blood."

Mike nods. "I think we need to do some research, figure out the cause and effect. I mean, there's got to be a power source, right?"

"What do you mean?"

"Something that's causing all of the magic. You know, in the Frankenstein story, the monster was brought to life with lightning. The lightning was the power source."

I nod slowly, considering this. "So we need to find out what's allowing the Oldies to upgrade?"

"Yeah. Find the source, destroy the source, stop the Oldies." He loudly slurps the last of the milkshake. "Simple."

"Yeah, real simple," I mutter. I nod to the empty glass. "And way to share!"

"You said you weren't hungry."

"Let's just go."

Mike pays the check with some crumpled bills from his pocket, and together we make our way back into the hot sun.

"The power source has to be close to Goodie Lane, right?" he says. "Why else would they live there for so long?"

At this I grab his arm. "The pond! They were talking about the pond. Attwood's going there tonight."

Mike's eyes light up. "And didn't Red say he saw them once in the pond? At midnight? And their stitches disappeared—"

"*And* that's where Mary Hove went missing," I add, feeling breathless.

"That must be the key, Parker! The power source."

"So let's go check it out." I start toward the woods, but Mike pulls my arm.

"Not now, Parker. Midnight. When Attwood is doing her thing. We've got to catch them in the act."

I stare in the direction of the pond, considering Mike's words before finally nodding. "Fine. Tonight."

I try to take a nap after dinner so that I'll be at my best once midnight strikes, but it's useless. I toss and turn, play with my phone, try to read a book, and finally give up.

Around nine o'clock, Mom pokes her head in my door. "Hey. You've been cooped up in here for hours. Want to come and watch a show with me?"

I hesitate before answering, not sure if I have it in me to sit beside her for an hour and pretend that everything is OK.

She rests her head against the doorframe. "I'll make choco-pop," she says, tempting me with a smile.

Choco-pop is literally just salted popcorn with a drizzle of chocolate syrup on top. On the one hand, it's nothing fancy, but on the other hand, it is the most magical snack in the world.

"OK," I tell her, before following her downstairs.

We share a bowl of popcorn on the couch, with Billy stretched out in between us. My eyes glaze over looking at the screen for an hour. When the show ends, Mom gives me a kiss on the cheek and tells me that she's going to bed. She's got the first shift tomorrow morning. Before going up, she stops in the kitchen to make herself a cup of Grandma Jane's tea, which I know will have her passed out in no time. I stay downstairs, listening for each familiar sound of her getting ready for bed: changing, brushing her teeth, washing her face, finally calling Billy up to join her.

"Good night, boy," I tell him. He licks my hand before trotting up the stairs.

Once I hear my mom's door shut, I make my way back into my own bedroom to get ready for tonight. I jog in place, shaking out my limbs as my running playlist pulses loudly through my headphones. This is what I usually do before a big race: I warm up, get psyched, and try to focus. Only, what I'm going to do tonight is way more important than any track meet, or anything else I've ever done.

I don't stop moving until my muscles feel as if they're on fire, until it's time to go.

Once again, Mike and I agreed to wear all black, but this time, I tug on fitted training gear as opposed to Mom's old, baggy clothes. I need to make sure I'm ready to run if need be—I need to be ready for anything. I weave my hair into a single braid before stepping in front of the mirror. I catch a glimpse of a photograph of my dad, perched in the center of my dresser. He's smiling in it, his face full of light and dimples. People always used to tell us that we look alike, but nobody's said that to me since he died. I guess it's too painful, for them and for me.

I'm going to figure it all out, Dad.

I spin away from the photo as my eyes begin to water.

I turn instead to my jewelry box, pulling out a necklace that Grandma Jane gave me for my birthday this year. It has a simple chain with a rough green stone that turns a gold color when it hits the light. I don't usually dress up enough to wear it, but she told me it would keep me safe, and as silly as it sounds, I feel better having a piece of my grandma with me for what I'm about to do.

As soon as I clasp it around my neck, my phone buzzes on the bed.

The eagles have flown, Mike writes.

My heart beats faster as I type back: **ALL of the eagles?**

No, he answers, **just Bea and Attwood. Meet you outside.**

I take one last big breath before tiptoeing out of my room, down the stairs, and out of the house. Mike motions to me from behind the bush on the side of my porch. Like me, he's clad in black and looking nervous.

"Sup, Parker," he whispers. "They just went through the woods." He points to the edge of the cul-de-sac.

"We should stick by the bushes until we reach the trees," I say. "We don't want the other Oldies to see us."

"Agreed."

We take off through the night, ducking in and around a set of hedges until we reach the edge of the cul-de-sac. Up ahead, I can make out the backs of Ms. Bea and Ms. Attwood as they break off toward the pond. We follow them through the shadows until we're as close as we can safely be. Then, we hide beneath a set of oaks, the trees crisscrossing above our heads like an *X* marking our spot.

It's dark, so dark that my ears perk up, compensating for what my eyes can't see. But even in the blackness, I can still make out Ms. Bea's figure, draped in a long, hooded robe. She waves a hand in the air, and with that rapid motion, all of the clouds seem to clear away from the moon, as if her fingers were somehow able to pick them away like cobwebs. Attwood comes to her side, and they both face the water as their robes billow around them. The color is iridescent like a pearl, like the moon that now lights up the entire surface of the pond.

Ms. Bea waves her hands over the water, sending a series of ripples across the surface without even making contact. Tipping her face up toward the sky, she chants in a language that I've never heard. Ms. Attwood picks up on it, harmonizing with Bea's voice as if they're singing some ancient song. As they speak, the pond begins to glow, filling the space around it with a warm, orange light.

Bea nods to Attwood, who rolls up the sleeves of her

robe to reveal the freshly stitched shoulders. She takes Bea's hand before they lower themselves into the pond. Together, they close their eyes and continue chanting as the moon brightens, until the entire woods seem to be bathed in light. Mike and I shrink back against the trees, hoping that our dark clothing will be enough of a cover, and for a moment I'm afraid that the pounding of my heart will give us away. But they don't seem to notice us.

Their voices ring out louder and louder. The stitches on Attwood's arms begin to melt and disappear. The ritual goes on until a giant gust of wind circles the area, and Bea and Attwood cry out one last time. Then it's silent.

When they reopen their eyes, Attwood's arms are completely healed. The moon dips back behind the clouds, shrouding us in darkness, but the orange light from the pond continues to pulse beneath the surface like a heartbeat.

Mike and I watch the Oldies climb out of the water. Their robes don't look the slightest bit wet or dirty, even though they were submerged in pond scum only moments before.

"How does it feel?" Ms. Bea asks.

Attwood shakes her arms and laughs. "Good as new, I should think." Bea tilts her head back and laughs, too, only her laugh sounds different than Attwood's: Bea's is much deeper, with an edge to it that sounds positively sinister. It causes me to tighten my grip on the tree, digging my fingernails into the bark.

The two women walk away from the pond with their elbows linked together. Each step they take is a step closer to Mike and me. I bite my lip and try to keep my breaths even, squeezing my body against the trunk. *Please don't see us... Please don't see us...*

Ms. Bea turns her head slightly, casting her eyes in my direction, sending icicles through my bones. Does she know we're here? I close my eyes, wishing them away.

"I sure could use a cup of tea," Ms. Attwood says, her voice cutting through the darkness.

The simple statement is enough to make me reopen my eyes. I watch as Bea spins away from us, refocusing her attention on Attwood. "Come to my house. I'll make you a special cup before bed. My mother's recipe."

"That would be lovely, Beatrice. Thank you—for the tea, and of course, for all of this." Ms. Attwood gestures to her own body.

Ms. Bea winks at her. "What else are friends for?"

To my relief, they continue to walk past Mike and me, with Bea humming as they move. She throws one last look over her shoulder, and then pulls down her hood before the two women disappear through the woods and back toward Goodie Lane.

I hear Mike exhale to my left. "That. Was. Wild!"

My heart is still racing. "Do you think they saw us?"

"No."

"Not even Bea?"

"No way. She would have tried to grab us or something if she knew we were here. Especially given what we just saw. I mean, look." He waves to the pond. "It's still glowing."

I turn and follow his gaze, and the warmth from the light instantly relaxes my body. I take it as a sign. "Mary Hove," I mutter.

"What?"

"It's her. It must be her . . ."

"Parker, what are you—"

I'm already moving toward the pond before he can finish his sentence, not stopping until I'm standing at the edge of the murky water.

When the weather gets hotter, the pond scum gets thicker, greener, and somehow more ominous, especially on this side of the park, where the full trees stretch over the edges, creating a dark shade.

"Mary?" I call, stretching my toes over the edge. A flutter moves beneath the surface, until the ripples part and long tendrils of black hair unroll, exposing a pretty, heart-shaped face, with doll-like lips and a smile that is comforting despite the grayish tone of her translucent skin.

"Parker!" Mike cries. "What are you doing?" At once he is at my side, looking panicked.

"Did you see her?" I ask.

"See who? What are you talking about?"

"The face—the woman. Right there!" I point to the water, but the face is gone.

Mike shakes his head. "I think we should—"

I wave him off. "*Shh! I hear something.*" I hold my breath and listen. On cue, a soft humming sounds in the water, almost like a whisper.

"I don't hear anything—"

"*Shh!*"

I strain my ears as the murmuring gets louder. The orange glow begins to pulsate once again beneath the algae; it throbs rhythmically. The tempo warms me. I want to be closer to it. My body unfolds. I feel weightless. I am floating.

And now I see it: a woman's severed hand gripping the orange light like a squished piece of fruit. The fingers then release the light and reach for me like claws.

"*Parker!*"

I gasp and flap my arms wildly, unable to take a full breath before I plunge into the water. I beat my arms and legs furiously, but they feel odd, like I've forgotten how to swim.

But no, it's more than that. Someone, or something, is holding me under. I force my eyes open and see the ghost woman floating over me, only now her features look warped, like someone splashed water onto a fresh painting of a beautiful woman, making her appear monstrous. Her dark hair ties my limbs, holding me in place. My chest hurts. My whole body feels cold.

Suddenly, a large splash sends waves strong enough to shove away the woman. A new set of arms wraps around my waist, hoisting me up, and up, and out. When I open my eyes, Mike is hovering over me. I'm covered in pond scum, sprawled out on a pile of mud.

"Are you OK?" he asks, falling down beside me as we both gasp for air.

I don't answer. I don't know. I still can't seem to catch my breath. My whole body aches. And when I blink, all I see is that woman—that pretty face turning into a monster, a monster that just tried to kill me.

"You . . ." I start, letting my sentence fall off and disappear into the darkness.

"You don't have to talk right now," Mike says gently. "Let's just get you out of here."

He helps me to my feet. I turn around and search once more for the monster in the pond, but instead I see a single human hand, floating to the surface just beneath the fallen branch of the lightning tree. A wave of dizziness turns everything black, and the next time I open my eyes, Mike Warren is carrying me home.

CHAPTER 14

Red stares at us from across the library study room, his mouth a tight line. "Were you followed?"

"No," I say.

"Are you certain?"

"The Oldies are still on Goodie Lane," Mike says. "At least they were when we left."

Red nods as he folds his long fingers across his lap. I can't stop staring at his hands: the bony joints, the age spots, the curve of the knuckles, the deep lines. He catches me looking at them. "Are you all right, Quinn?"

"Your hands..." I try to shake off the memory of last night as Mike drags his chair closer to mine.

"It's OK. Tell Red what you saw," he says. "Tell him about the woman. About the hand."

I take a deep breath, wishing I could just forget the face, the hand, forget everything.

Because for the first time throughout this entire investigation, I'm genuinely scared. The fall in the pond did me in. I've never felt so out of control of my own body.

"*You could have drowned,*" Mike told me this morning as he walked me over to the library. "*Face it, I saved your life. I'm your Batman.*"

"*You're still not my Batman,*" I told him, even though he was right: he had saved my life.

"Come on, Parker, tell him," Mike urges now. "You're safe here."

"I thought it was Mary," I finally say, picturing the dark-haired woman in the water.

Red's face narrows. "My Mary? Mary Hove?"

I nod. "I thought she wanted to give me a clue. So I followed the light, and I saw a face. She was pretty," I continue, taking my time with each word, because the truth is so hard to say out loud. "She had dark hair, like Mary's, and she was smiling." I shiver. "Until she pulled me under."

Red leans forward, resting his elbows on his knees. "Then what happened?"

I feel my eyes start to tear up as I picture the twisted

mouth, the sharp, angular lines that left creases all over the demon's face, like scars. Mike places a hand on my shoulder and squeezes. I sniffle and continue.

"Her hair wrapped around my arms and legs. She was trying to drown me. Until—until . . ."

"Until I saved her," Mike says, grinning.

"Thank goodness you were with her," Red says. He puts his head in his hands. It looks as if he's aged ten more years over the last week. "And what about the severed hand?"

"I saw it twice," I explain. "Once just before I was pulled in. I saw it squeezing the orange light." I turn to Mike. "You really didn't see any of this?"

"Nope. Nothing. You ever see the light, Red?"

Red shakes his head, too. "Never. Only Mary saw it."

I look from one to the other. "Maybe I can see it because I live in her house?"

"Or maybe it's because of your dad?" Mike asks. "Like maybe you're somehow connected to the Oldies because one of them is wearing his leg?"

Red grimaces. "It doesn't matter. It's all part of the Oldies' trickery to lure you there. Monsters, that's what they are."

I won't argue with that. I don't think I will ever be able to look at water the same way after last night.

"Where did you see the hand the second time?" Red asks.

"After Mike pulled me out. I turned around, and I saw it floating on the surface, right under the lightning tree."

"The lightning tree?"

I gesture with my arms. "You know, the big one on the edge that looks like it's been struck by lightning? It sort of just hangs over the water now, kind of droopy."

"I know the one," Red says.

"What if it's the power source?" Mike asks.

"What?"

"The hand that Quinn saw, what if it's the thing that we need to destroy in order to stop the Oldies?"

Red isn't buying it. "No, it's too easy. Why would the Oldies show you their weakness right there in the open?"

I stare at him. "Because maybe they thought I'd be dead." I turn to Mike. "Maybe Bea *did* see us as they were leaving. The song she was humming sounded like the same song that was coming from the water—maybe it was part of her spell. Magic." I sit up tall in the wooden chair. "We need to go back there."

Red's face clouds over. "Out of the question!"

"But if Mike's right and that hand is the power source? Then it's our only shot at stopping them. Time is running out! Attwood and Smith mentioned the Fourth—"

"And they mentioned using Parker as a sacrifice," Mike adds. "As much as I hate the idea, I think Parker's right: we need to go fishing."

"Absolutely not," Red says sternly. "It's dangerous for you two to go back to that pond. They're obviously setting you up, tricking you into drowning. Don't you remember the threats?"

"I really think I'm meant to follow the light. Not the face, but the light. I think it'll lead me to the hand."

"Or your death."

"If the Oldies wanted me dead, I'd be gone already," I argue. "Besides, it's not like I'd go alone."

At this, Mike puffs out his chest. "Yeah, she's got me." He flexes his biceps. "And all this." I whack him in the arm.

Red rises to his feet. "If this is the plan, then you can count me out."

Mike and I exchange looks.

"What?!"

"You can't leave Operation Ghost Hunter—we need you!"

"It's not without a heavy heart," Red says, turning at the door, "but you kids are playing with a fire more dangerous than you understand, and I can't . . . I won't sit around and support it."

With this, he slips out of the study room, leaving Mike and me alone.

Mike waits a beat and then shrugs. "Looks like it's just us again."

"You got any fishing rods?"

. . .

The plan is to wait until tomorrow afternoon to return to the pond. But the next morning, Mike shows up at my front door.

"Sorry, Mrs. Parker. I hope I didn't wake you up."

"Nonsense, Michael. I'm getting used to these little visits." She waves him inside. "You want breakfast?"

"I'd love some milk. Thank you, Mrs. Parker," Mike says with a smile.

Mom gestures to me. "Quinn, can you pour him a glass? I have to get showered. Early shift, remember?" Armed with her coffee, she shuffles upstairs.

Billy settles at Mike's feet as I pour him a glass of milk. We pretend to talk about the weather until we hear the sound of the shower turning on.

I lean in close to him. "What's up? I thought we weren't meeting until later?"

His face turns serious. "I just saw Mrs. Smith go over to Bea's place."

"So?"

"So, that's not their routine. You know as well as I do that they wake up, drink tea, water their roses, and then go to work. They don't do social visits this early. Something must be up."

"Then let's go investigate," I hiss, standing up.

Together we dart across the street as quickly as possible to avoid detection. Even though we've done this before, it feels different now. We've seen so much more since the last time we burrowed ourselves in Ms. Bea's side rosebushes.

Once again, the thorns dig into my skin as we take our positions below the window, but thankfully, the window is actually open this time.

Ms. Bea is wearing something long and dramatic as usual, the floaty edges grazing the floor as she paces up and down the room. Mrs. Smith is perched on the sofa, holding a teacup with both hands.

"All Angela said," Mrs. Smith is explaining, "is that the spell doesn't seem to be working as well these days."

Ms. Bea's pace quickens, the train of her dress jutting out behind her as she turns. "The *nerve* of her to complain," she snaps. "After all I've done for her over the centuries."

"Oh, Beatrice," Mrs. Smith coos, "it's not like that. She appreciates your hard work. We all do—"

"Well, it doesn't sound like it. I gave her a job. I gave her a husband, a life. I gave her—I gave all of you—*immortality*."

Mrs. Smith places her teacup down on the coffee table. "Now, Beatrice. There's no need to be so upset—"

"I saved each and every one of you!" Ms. Bea goes on, the steps becoming more urgent and forceful. "Using my dear mother's spell to bring justice to the Goodie name, which this town soiled the day they burned her at the stake."

She flicks her wrist toward the portrait hanging above the sofa, the painting of the pretty woman with the dark hair.

And it hits me. That was never Mary Hove in the water—
it was Ms. Bea's mother! Shivers pulse down my spine as I
struggle to hold on to the windowsill.

"Or have you all forgotten?" Bea demands.

"No, Beatrice. Of course not."

"It's been over three hundred years," she continues, "and
not a day goes by that I don't relive that night, watching my
mother burn, feeling the flames against my face as they held
me there, forcing me to watch. She was strong, though—she
was a force! My mother tried to fight back, sending fire from
her right hand toward her accusers, but instead the flame
missed and hit the tree. That blasted tree. It taunts me every
time I see it . . ."

The lightning tree!

Mrs. Smith clicks her tongue sympathetically as Ms.
Bea studies the portrait of her mother. "They called her a
witch, you know. *Sarah Goodie, the Witch of South Haven.*"
Her eyes narrow. "Such a lie!"

Mrs. Smith clenches her teeth. "Well, not really a lie,
Beatrice, dear. She *was* a witch . . ."

"But she was a *good* witch. She healed people. She
extended life. That's all I'm trying to do."

Mrs. Smith shrugs one shoulder and picks up her tea
again. "Then what about the girl?"

I can't help but gasp as the conversation turns to me.

Ms. Bea stops pacing. "A necessity to the cause, I'm

afraid." Her face hardens. "If you want the spell to have more power, we need a sacrifice. It's been years since the last one."

"It just seems like such a shame," Mrs. Smith says. "Think of her poor mother, losing both a husband and a daughter in a little over a year. And the girl is nice enough. Reminds me of Mary Hove. Only, this one is younger, isn't she?" She clicks her tongue before sipping her tea.

"Her youth will help the magic." Ms. Bea shrugs. "But . . . if you'd prefer to leave well enough alone, I can skip the sacrifice and downsize the spell to one."

Mrs. Smith's eyes widen. "What do you mean?"

"Well, the spell would be ten times more powerful if I just used it on myself. Which I have a good mind to do if you lot keep complaining about my methods and abilities."

At this, Mrs. Smith waves her hands in the air. "No, no, Beatrice. No one is against you. We are forever in your debt. Whatever you need to get ready for the anniversary, we're all on board to help. The Fourth of July is *your* day. Always will be."

This seems to appease Ms. Bea, who smiles slightly. "The Fourth of July is *our* day." She then takes a seat beside Mrs. Smith on the couch, her dress fanned out around her. They sip their tea, and their conversation turns to mundane things: the weather, the roses, and how much they're both looking forward to the fireworks.

Mike and I exchange looks before sliding down into the bushes. He motions to the street, and I follow him away from Bea's window, crossing back over Goodie Lane until we reach his house.

"Come in," he tells me. "Mom and Dad are at work."

He leads me through a front foyer—that's strewn with shoes, umbrellas, and a collection of Mike's many Yankees hats—and into the living room. It looks more like a library, with wall-to-wall bookcases overflowing with textbooks, novels, and binders labeled DISSERTATION, whatever that means. The room itself smells like hazelnut coffee and feels quite cozy, with navy walls and a big couch that looks like it would swallow you whole as soon as you sat down. Family photos are positioned every which way: smiling faces of Mike and his parents throughout the years. I realize that it's my first time ever being in the Warrens' house.

"What are we doing here?" I ask.

He goes toward one of the bookcases, his eyes set into game mode. "Research."

I stand back and take a series of deep, deliberate breaths as he searches the titles for who knows what. It's hard to let everything from the last few days sink in.

"Let me get this straight," I finally say, rubbing my temples with my fingers. "Ms. Bea's a—a *witch*?"

Mike snorts. "Really, Parker? *That's* the only part that's throwing you? Not the part about the human sacrifice, or the demon that tried to drown you? Not the fact that the fountain of youth is practically in our own backyards?"

"It's—it's just . . ." I trail off, lost for words.

Mike throws me a look. "Why are you so shocked? You called all this supernatural stuff from the beginning."

"Yeah, but I never thought there would be this much!" I study Mike's calm face. "Why are you so cool with this? How are you not freaking out at all?"

Mike gives a slight shrug. "I like science," he admits. "Science is all about evidence. I got my evidence."

"It's that simple?"

"Nothing about this is *simple*." He turns back to the bookcase. "Which is why we have to be smart about our plan."

"What are you looking for?"

"South Haven history books. My parents are historians. They must have something from the 1600s . . ." He yanks a book from the shelf. "Jackpot!"

I follow him toward the kitchen, where we sit side by side at the wooden table. Like the living room, the kitchen is painted in shades of blue, and a pile of books is balanced in the middle of the table like an impromptu centerpiece.

"I just want to see if there really was a Sarah Goodie," he explains, flipping through the pages until he gets to the index.

"You don't believe Bea's story?"

"I do, but, you know. Science. Got to find the evidence." He offers a weak smile as he runs his finger down the letters, stopping on G. He then flips to the appropriate page, turning the book toward me so that I can read alongside him.

"It's true. Look! Sarah Goodie really was burned at the stake just like Bea said. And then they drowned her in the pond afterward."

"Why would they do that?" I ask. "Didn't she die in the fire?"

"Insurance, I guess. I think double executions were common if they thought you were a witch." He continues reading. "Sarah was twenty-seven years old at the time. It says that her right hand was severed from her burning body after she tried to curse the crowd. The hand was tossed into the pond separately from the rest of her remains." He flips the page. "And here's a sketch done of her."

I lean in and gasp at the face staring back at me: the tendrils of long, black hair, inkblot eyes, heart-shaped face, and pretty smile. It's the woman from the painting in Bea's living room, the monster from the pond.

I slam the book shut, breathing hard.

Mike pushes the book away and gets me a glass of water and a packet of cookies. "Do you want some Oreos?" he asks. "You know, in case you're in shock."

"I'm not in shock!"

He squints at me. "You sure? You're looking kind of

clammy, Parker." He waves the cookies under my nose. I grab one and stuff it into my mouth, practically choking on the sweetness.

"Happy?"

"Very."

I force myself to swallow, drowning what's left of the cookie with my glass of water. "Can we just make a plan? We're running out of time."

Mike sits back down. "What are you thinking?"

"The hand must be the key."

Mike grins. "Called it." He tries to high-five me, but I leave him hanging.

"Since the hand was the last thing Sarah used for her curse, it must be the key to her power—to Bea's power."

"So we go to the fireworks first," Mike says. "Let the Oldies see us. Make them think that we're going to watch the whole show."

"Then we duck back to the pond and get the hand."

"*I'll* get the hand. You stay far away from that water witch. I don't need to risk tetanus trying to save you again. That pond was *nasty!*"

"It'll be fine," I insist, clenching my fists. "I know what we're up against now. I won't go too close. And besides, we'll be using a fishing rod."

Mike laughs. "I thought you were kidding with that whole fishing pole thing."

"Well, how else do *you* suggest we pull the hand up?"

"I guess you're lucky that I'm an ace fisherman, then."

"When have you ever been fishing?" I ask.

"Every weekend. You know, before Dad got promoted." His voice softens a bit at this, and I start to realize how much Mr. Warren's new job must be affecting Mike.

There's an awkward silence, before I shift and ask, "What do we do with the hand once we get it?"

"We have to destroy it."

"But *how*?"

"I don't know," Mike admits.

I think for a moment, replaying Ms. Bea's words in my head. "Fire," I whisper. "Bea said they burned her mother back in the day, so that means fire started the spell—"

"And fire has to end it." Mike flashes a cheeky smile. "Wow, I'm kind of impressed, Parker."

"With what?"

"Your powers of deduction."

I sigh and stand up. "I don't even know what that means. You're being weird, again."

"You know, like Sherlock Holmes."

At this I raise an eyebrow. "So if I'm Sherlock, then you're Watson? *You're* the sidekick?" I smile.

He frowns. "No! No way. I'm the hero, not the—"

"Robin!"

"Don't you dare!"

I laugh. "Face it, Mike. I'm *your* Batman!" Without giving him a chance to argue, I stuff another cookie into my mouth.

Mike gives a slight smile. "Touché, Parker."

"What about our friends?" I ask after a moment.

"What about them?"

"Zoe and I have been going to the fireworks together since we were five. She's expecting me to go with her and the other girls."

"So? This is way more important than tradition."

"But it'll look really suspicious if we don't go like normal. Don't your friends want you to go with them?"

"Yeah, but I already told them I'm busy."

"Well, text them back and say you'll go with them. The Oldies need to see us there with a group of people. They need to think that we're just having a normal night like every other kid in town."

"But then what do we do with our friends? Ditch them?"

I bite my lip before answering, feeling the guilt in the pit of my stomach, which makes me wish that I didn't eat so many Oreos. "I can't think of another way," I say. "Can you?"

Mike shakes his head. "OK, so we go to the fireworks like normal. Make sure we see the Oldies there and make sure they see us. Then as soon as it all begins, we ditch our friends and meet at the edge of the beach."

"Wear your running shoes," I tell him, "so we can run to the pond and back, hopefully before the Oldies notice."

"We probably have around two hours when all is said and done."

"Is that enough time?"

Mike throws up his hands. "It's all we got."

"And if we fail?"

"Then we call the police," Mike says firmly. "Whether they believe us or not, we have to. Agreed?"

I gulp. "Agreed."

That night, I dream about the pond. In my dream, it's dark and foggy. It must have rained the night before, because the ground is coated in mud. My sneakers stick and pop with each step. Mike is with me somewhere, but it's too dark to see him. The smell of sulfur and rotten eggs is strong and nauseating, and it's coming from the water. The orange light glows. I walk toward it and feel that familiar warmth all over my body. I crouch down under the lightning tree, extending my arms between the rocks along the edge of the pond. Closer . . . closer . . . The water moves beneath my gaze. It whispers my name, calling me toward it. My fingers skim the surface, and suddenly *something*—or someone—grabs ahold of my hand from within the water, pulling me over the rocks and down into the murk and the scum and the darkness. I'm screaming, and choking, and fighting to free myself, but the hand grips me tighter, drags me lower until I can no longer see, or feel, or hope.

I wake with a racing heart, the tears mixing with the sweat on my face and neck. Billy jumps onto the bed to lick my cheek. I reach for the phone.

"Grandma Jane?"

"Honey pie!" she exclaims. She doesn't ask me what's wrong or why I'm calling so late. And I love her even more for it.

"Did I wake you?" I ask.

"Nonsense. I can never sleep after my bingo tournaments, you know that."

I smile. "Did you win?"

"Quinnie, I *dominated*. Four games in a row! Miranda was convinced that I was cheating, but honestly—who cheats at bingo? Can you imagine?"

"No, Grandma."

"Anyhoo, I need to dig up my recipe book before I go to bed. I'm waking up early to bake you your favorite chocolate cake."

My stomach rumbles. "Really? For what? It's not my birthday."

"Didn't your mother tell you, dear? Your aunt Jennifer and aunt Rebecca are taking her to the casino for an overnight. I'm in charge! We'll get pizza and eat our weight in cake . . ."

She continues to ramble. Her words are enough to calm me down, and I fall asleep with the phone still by my ear.

By the time morning comes, I've shifted into battle mode, suiting up in my traditional red, white, and blue attire: red-striped tank top, white pull-up socks, denim cutoffs. Zoe and I have been wearing an outfit like this to the fireworks since we were kids.

I spend the rest of the morning helping Mom find what she needs for her trip. When she's finally upstairs packing her overnight bag, I sneak out into Mike's garage and help him find all of his dad's fishing equipment. Carefully, we prop two poles and a tackle box beside the garage, right next to the charcoal barbecue. I then run back to my house to pack a bag. *What do you need to take down a witch?* I settle on a flashlight, matches, mini sand shovel, plastic bags, gloves, a pack of gummy bears, and a bottle of water. I throw it all into my backpack, before stealing a peek out the living room window.

Ms. Bea is watering her roses for the fourth time today. She suddenly turns her body toward me and smiles with her painted red lips. Her eyes, however, remain hollow and mean. Billy starts to growl from the sofa, but I force myself to smile and wave. After a pause, Ms. Bea waves back stiffly.

"Oh, there you are," Mom says, dropping her overnight

bag by the door. "You girls have your normal plans for tonight?"

"Yeah, just the usual," I lie, smiling weakly.

"Well, Grandma Jane will be here by six. Pizza money is on the table, if you and Zoe get hungry. What time are you heading to the fireworks?"

"Probably around seven."

We both jump as the doorbell rings.

"I bet it's Michael again," Mom says, opening the door. "I feel like he lives here lately!"

But I'm surprised to find Zoe already standing on the stoop. Like me, she's wearing her cutoffs, striped tank, and white socks, and she's armed with two tote bags.

"Hi, Mrs. Parker," she says cheerfully. "Happy Fourth!"

"Zoe! Come in, honey. You girls look adorable."

Zoe shrugs. "Tradition." She thrusts one of the bags toward me.

"What's this?" I ask.

"Supplies."

I peer inside the bag and see face paint, glitter, and ribbons galore. I raise an eyebrow at her. "For real?"

She nods. "I take my holidays very seriously. I was thinking we could invite Lex and Kaylee over to get festive before we leave for the fireworks."

"That works." I turn to my mom. "Can I have extra friends over for pizza?"

Mom shrugs. "You know Grandma Jane won't mind—the more the merrier, as far as she's concerned. I'll leave some extra cash. Order what you want from Cucina Della Nonna. Just make sure that you clean up your mess, and come home right after the fireworks. No ifs, ands, or buts!"

"I know, Mom."

"Don't give me side-eye," Mom says. "I just want my girl safe."

My stomach tightens.

"Where are you going, Mrs. Parker?" Zoe asks, noticing Mom's bag.

"Oh, my sisters are dragging me to the casino for the night. Didn't Quinn tell you?"

"I guess I forgot," I admit.

Mom comes over and gives me a tight squeeze around the shoulders. "My baby girl. I'll miss you. Call me if you need anything. I can come home like that." She snaps her fingers.

"OK, OK, Mom." I feel my face turning pink, but she hugs me again and I feel my body relax in her arms.

I wish I could tell her about what's been going on, about tonight, but I don't want her to worry. Or for her to think I've lost my mind.

Zoe and I follow Mom to the door. "Remember," she says, "be home right after the fireworks. That means that by ten o'clock sharp, you are walking through this door." She nods as she opens it and steps out onto the landing.

I look across the street. Ms. Bea's still there watching us, watching my mom kiss me goodbye and stuff her suitcase into the car and drive away. Then Ms. Bea waves to me, slowly, like a beauty queen in a pageant. Billy starts to bark and I have to hold him by the collar so that he doesn't bolt across the street.

"Let's go," Zoe says, pulling us both back inside.

I double-lock the door, only unlatching the bolt again once Lex and Kaylee arrive, armed with snacks and even more glitter.

I text Mike when they're not looking: **How are you doing?**

Good, he writes. **I see the girls are there.**

Stalker, I type back. I think for a minute and then add, **Want to come for pizza? You can bring Max and Nolan. 6:00.**

He sends back a thumbs-up. The girls are staring at me as I tuck my phone away.

"Who are you texting?" Zoe asks, eyeing me suspiciously. "And don't say your mom. I know she's driving."

"Yeah, and the rest of us are here," Lex adds.

I join them on the bed, pushing a roll of Oreos and a sparkly ribbon out of the way. Lex picks up the ribbon and begins weaving it through my ponytail.

"I invited Mike and his friends to meet us here for pizza,"

I admit. "And I think they're going to come to the fireworks with us."

Zoe doesn't bother to hide her pout. "But this is supposed to be a girl's thing. It's tradition."

"I know, I'm sorry. I just thought that we could, you know, all go together. As friends."

Kaylee raises an eyebrow. *"Friends?"*

"Friends."

Zoe lets out an exaggerated sigh. "OK, I guess that's cool. But they've got to wear glitter. Them's the rules."

I laugh. It feels good to laugh for a change, especially on a day like this. That's one of the many things I love about Zoe: she can make anyone smile. We paint red and blue stars on each other's cheeks and shoulders until Grandma Jane arrives in her bright blue VW Beetle. She beeps the horn about a dozen times, causing the girls and me to come out of hiding to help her with her bags.

"My beautiful girls," she exclaims, pulling me into a hug. "How gorgeous you all look—and so *festive*. I made banana bread. Here, take this." She hands me a warm tin covered in aluminum foil. "And one for you, with chocolate chips instead of nuts." She hands a second tin to Zoe, who takes it greedily. "Your mother called me from the road. She said you're having some more friends over for dinner, is that right?"

"If that's OK with you," I answer.

"The more the merrier! I'm just glad that I decided to double the recipe for this cake. Do your other friends like chocolate?"

Zoe takes the cake and stacks it on top of her banana bread tin. "Who *doesn't* like chocolate?"

"That's what I thought! For heaven's sake, what are you looking at, Quinn?" Grandma Jane follows my gaze over to Ms. Bea, watering her roses yet again, still watching us. Grandma Jane huffs. "Anyone teach you that it's impolite to stare?" she shouts across the street.

Ms. Bea flashes Grandma Jane a nasty look but puts her watering can down and disappears inside.

I gasp. "She listened to you!"

"Well, of course, dear. I'm a force to be reckoned with, don't you know?" She laughs and puts her arms around me, leading us up the stairs. "Now, how about we take a sample of that chocolate cake before the rest of your friends get here? I'm famished!"

We eat about half of the chocolate cake before Mike and his friends arrive for dinner, and then collectively we polish it off before the pizza is delivered. Together, we devour two large pizzas and a side order of Cucina Della Nonna's famous garlic sticks. We laugh and talk while we eat. I'm having such a good time that I almost forget about the mission.

That is, until the clock strikes seven.

"You kids better get a move on if you want to get a good seat for those fireworks," Grandma Jane says after we've cleaned up. She's arranged a pile of old blankets for us to take to sit on and an extra-large spray bottle. "The beach is so gnatty at night this time of year," she says, handing me the bottle. "Take some of my homemade bug spray."

I sniff the contents, and it actually smells really great, as if Grandma Jane somehow managed to capture the essence of chocolate cake and rosemary oil. "You sure this is bug spray?" I ask. "It smells delicious!"

"Just make sure you spray it all over you and your friends," she tells me. "I made it especially for you for tonight."

I tuck it into my backpack. "Thanks, Grandma."

"You're welcome, Quinnie." She puts her hands on my shoulders, bending slightly over to meet my eyes. "Are you sure you don't want to stay home? We can watch the fireworks from the porch. We'll still be able to see them from here."

I look deep into her worried eyes, and I can't help but wonder how much she knows. "I wish I could, Grandma, but I have to go."

She gives my shoulders a squeeze before releasing me. "Just be home right after." She follows us to the door and blows us all kisses as we head out.

Mike and I exchange determined looks, and together we start walking. I can feel the Oldies watching us from their windows, but when I look up, there's no one there.

The seven of us are loud as we tramp down Goodie Lane, and even louder as we make our way to the beach at the other end of town. I pretend to laugh along with my friends, pretend to care about all of the silly little things that we talk about, but my mind is on one thing: the pond.

The beach itself is already crowded, with half of the town stretched out across the sand on blankets and lawn chairs, innocently sipping on drinks and nibbling on snacks. I'm jealous of how blissfully unaware they all are about the darkness lurking just a few miles away.

Zoe and I unpack her bags of supplies and blankets, and we all make camp by the shore. It isn't long before the sun starts to disappear behind the waves, changing the sky to an eerie shade of purple. I take out Grandma Jane's home-made bug spray and begin spritzing myself and everyone around me.

"Ugh, why are you spraying all that stuff on us?" Lex cries.

"Grandma Jane said it would keep the bugs away."

"It's making us smell sweet. The bugs are going to think we're dessert!" Zoe says, swatting me away.

I ignore them and keep on spraying. For some reason, I find the smell comforting. It helps me maintain composure, even when Mike leans over and whispers in my ear, "They're here."

A sharp chill slices through my spine as I slowly turn my head, taking in the Oldies. They move together as if in slow motion, fanning out their blankets in the sand. It's a funny image, seeing them so dressed up, sitting cross-legged on the ground just like the rest of us. Mr. Brown opens up a bottle of what looks like champagne, and together they raise their plastic glasses to the sky.

"What do you think they're celebrating?" Mike hisses.

I look at him. "What do you *think*?"

Their position couldn't be more perfect. They're stationed with their backs to us, far enough down the beach for us to see them, but for them to not see us.

"We need to go," Mike says.

I'm already standing up, ready to run.

"Where are you two off to?" Zoe asks as we stand.

"Bathroom," Mike and I answer in unison. Even I can hear how totally suspicious we sound as we shift together, staring nervously at our friends.

Mike's friend Nolan bursts out laughing. "Yeah right," he says between breaths. "Have fun, you two!"

"It's not like that—" I start to say, but suddenly Mike's arm is around my shoulders.

"We'll be back," he says, leading me away in the opposite direction of our friends, and more important, the Oldies.

We walk until we hit the main road, where we both break out into a hard run, flying as though we're in the race of our lives. The streets are empty. Everyone is at the fireworks, even the Oldies, which makes Goodie Lane feel all the more still and unsettling as we dip between Mike's house and mine.

Billy must sense us as we sneak around to the garage. I can hear him whining at the window and Grandma Jane's voice calling him over to her for a biscuit. I readjust my backpack over my shoulders and hand Mike the tackle box. We both take a fishing rod and quietly make our way toward the trees.

My knees seem to shake the closer we get to the pond. The grass surrounding the pond is saturated, strewn with puddles and mud, and an eerie mist hovers over the surface of the water. I half expect to hear the humming again, to see the ghostly face peering up through the algae. But so far, it's silent except for the buzzing of the gnats flying around our heads.

"Don't worry, the mist isn't as scary as it looks," Mike says, trying to reassure me. "It's just from the humidity. My dad told me that the last time we went night fishing."

We stand on the edge of the pond, just under the lightning tree.

"I've never been fishing before," I admit. "Is that weird? What do you do, anyway?"

"It's easy. You just . . ." He fumbles with the large hook and jabs himself in the finger. "Ouch!"

"I thought you were a *master fisherman*? Isn't that what you called yourself?"

"Hey, give me a break. I'm nervous."

I wait a beat before admitting, "Me too."

He casts the line just under the bent branch, which looks like a broken arm, reaching to the water.

"How are you supposed to hook a dead hand?" I ask. "Don't you need bait?"

"I'm hoping that you're the bait," he says. "I'm kind of banking on that pond witch reaching out for you again, and then I can hook her." He jerks the line a bit, sending ripples through the water before letting it fall still. We wait for two minutes that feel like forever.

"Nothing's happening." Mike narrows his eyes. "Do you see anything? The orange light?"

"No. Nothing."

I begin to feel the weight of the time ticking in my chest. Our silence makes every single noise sound even louder in comparison. Every time a squirrel steps on a branch or an owl hoots or the pond ripples, I can't help but jump inside my own skin.

But then suddenly, there's a real noise: a sound of footsteps crunching in the leaves behind us—*one, two, three*— and then just as quickly, it stops.

Mike's eyes widen as he hands me his pole. "Stay here, Parker. I'm going to check it out."

Before I can protest, Mike darts off, leaving me with nothing but my nerves and my backpack. I chew frantically on a piece of stale gum, waiting for a signal. I can't even see which way he ran through this mist, which seems to be getting denser by the second.

You're OK, I tell myself. *You're OK, you're OK, you're OK...*

The lightning tree appears extra illuminated this evening, but so far there's no orange light.

I whisper-yell for Mike but get no reply. I want to get this over with. I want to be back in my house with Grandma Jane, eating banana bread and watching something silly on TV.

"Mike, hurry up!"

Still no answer. I quickly search the clearing but see nothing. *It's now or never*, I tell myself, and trudge back over to the tree.

With each step I feel warmer and stickier. In moments, I'm standing at the edge of the pond in the same spot where I fell in. I squint into the water, desperate to see any sign of movement. I bend down and lean forward, my knees nestled in the mud, the ominous branches of the lightning tree hovering over my back. Cautiously, I reach out my hand. As soon as it makes contact with the water, a soft orange light begins to glow beneath my fingertips, drawing me toward it. And all of a sudden, I know that if I lean just a little bit farther, I'll find the hand.

But what if it's a trick? What if Sarah Goodie is lurking nearby, ready to pull me under as soon as I get close? I need Mike to spot me. I need him here just in case she tries to drag me down again.

"Mike!" I whisper-yell. "Mi-chael!" I'm answered in silence by the still and heavy air.

I crouch forward, my fingers gripping the pond grass. I rattle my head back and forth, trying to fight the gnats without giving myself away to the larger creatures hiding in the dark.

A twig snaps behind me. My stomach drops as I realize that I'm out of time. I can't wait for Mike. I have to lean in. Now!

My hand plunges toward the rocks just as the ripples start to form at the far end of the pond, signaling that Sarah Goodie has woken up. The hair comes into view first, sprawled out around her ghastly gray face, which is twisted and stretched, poking up from the water that is now so orange, it looks like fire. The skin on her body is charred and burned, and I can feel the heat and the anger rolling off of her. My heart beats faster as my fingers grope the edge of the pond, slipping across rocks and sand, and I don't want to know what else. I hear her hissing, I see her fangs.

"Mike!" I cry.

And just as I start to think that it's too late, that I've failed, my fingers land on something that doesn't feel like mud. It's smooth and heavy and so very cold. It's the hand! I squeeze it with everything I have and fall backward, scooting far away from the edge of the pond and a howling Sarah Goodie, who remains trapped in the very place where she was once executed. I pull myself to my feet and bolt through the darkness, away from the pond, through the woods, just running, running, running. I don't stop until I reach my house, and only then do I dare turn around. I hadn't known I was being followed, but one by one, they come forward.

CHAPTER 15

"Well, if it isn't Quinn Parker." Ms. Bea smirks at me with her bloodred lips. She is leading the pack of Oldies toward me. They walk slowly, like zombies, as if they don't have a care in the world, white robes covering their putty-like skin. "Looking for this?" She dangles my cell phone in the air. The other Oldies laugh. I dart to the locked door and call for Grandma Jane.

"Please, Grandma, hurry!"

Ms. Bea laughs louder. "That old wench is asleep on the couch with her hearing aid switched off. She can't hear you."

I continue to yell. I realize I'm still holding the hand. I catch the Browns staring at it. The Oldies move closer.

"You shouldn't have interfered, pretty girl," Ms. Bea continues. "We warned you. We warned Mary, too. She didn't listen. And neither did you!" She sucks her teeth in mock sadness. "They never listen, do they?"

The other Oldies laugh and agree: children never listen.

"Now, be a good girl," Ms. Bea tells me. "And give me back my mother's hand."

"Par-*ker*!"

Mike bolts toward us, whipping his backpack from side to side like a weapon. He knocks straight into Mr. Brown, who collapses onto the pavement. Mike keeps swinging.

"You're a little late," Ms. Bea says dryly. She snatches Mike's swinging bag, tossing it to the side. Mr. Brown gets back on his feet and wrestles Mike to the ground. I take a few steps forward to help, but then freeze as Mike screams at me.

"Don't move, Parker!"

I feel the tears on my face, and I don't know what to do. I can hear Billy barking his head off from the inside of my house.

I hold the slimy, cold hand up high above my head. "I'll give this back if you let him go."

Ms. Bea smiles at me, amused. "Of course you will, dear."

"I'm serious. Just let him go, please."

"I'm fine, Parker," Mike cries under Mr. Brown's weight. "Don't give it to them!"

"Enough!" a voice cries, cutting through the darkness.

Ms. Bea suddenly spins around. "Oh, Red. I was wondering when you'd show up. Late to the game, as usual. Just like with your precious Mary."

"I'm unarmed," he says, holding up his naked hands as he approaches. "Please stop this. Just let them go. They're children."

"Maybe you should have thought of that *before* recruiting them to spy on us," Ms. Bea says.

"You're right," Red says, still coming forward. "So take me instead of them. It's all my fault, just take me."

Ms. Bea scoffs. "Take you? What would we do with you? It's that pretty little one up there who we need. The one holding my hand."

"I told you," I yell, waving the hand in the air above my head. "It's yours. Just let Mike go and it's yours."

Ms. Bea cocks one of her perfect eyebrows at me. She looks like a store mannequin in the moonlight. "And how do I know you won't just whip out those matches you have in your bag and set it aflame? Hmm?"

How does she know I have matches?

She smiles at me as if reading my thoughts. "Lucky guess, dear. Now hand it over."

I take off my backpack and toss it into the street, still holding the hand. "Just let him go."

Fireworks crack above us, a gorgeous show of glitter and gold, patriotic streamers, and flowers in the thick night air.

"Oh look, you've made us miss our fireworks. We haven't missed a fireworks display in fifty years."

"Beautiful, aren't they, Beatrice?" says Dr. Smith.

"Always are." She sighs and looks back at me. "Now give me back my mother's hand."

I'm trembling, but I stand my ground. "Let my friend go."

"You first, dear."

I shake my head stubbornly. "No. You."

Ms. Bea watches the fireworks as she considers my proposal.

I have no clue what I'm doing. I shouldn't have tossed over the matches. I should have just burned the hand when I had the chance. Now, even if I give her the hand and she lets us go, they could still come after us later.

"Oh, fine," Ms. Bea says. She nods to Mr. Brown. "Let them go." She looks at me. "Go on. Join them."

I dart down the steps, making my way over to Mike and Red.

Ms. Bea arches a brow my way. "Now, be a good girl. Give it to me."

I look back and forth between Mike and Red. Their eyes plead for me not to, but what choice do I have? "I have to," I tell them. "I'm sorry, guys." I'm about to toss Bea the hand when I hear a strange rumbling noise behind me.

"Not so fast!"

I whip around to see Grandma Jane in all of her

nightgowned glory, dragging the charcoal barbecue from the side of the house to the front yard, stopping it with a screech on its rusty wheels. There's a bottle of lighter fluid in her nightgown pocket and she wastes no time pouring it over the grill, smiling wildly the whole time.

"You've got some nerve, Beatrice Goodie," she hollers. "Messing with my granddaughter." She pulls out a pack of matches from her other pocket.

"What are you doing?" Ms. Bea cries, showing her fear for the first time. The fireworks continue to boom overhead.

Grandma Jane looks up. "Oh, how lovely. Looks like the finale is starting." She grins as she drops a lit match onto the barbecue. I can feel the heat from the flames as they shoot up and dance.

"Throw it, Parker," Mike urges.

"I can't." If I throw it and it falls, one of the Oldies will snatch it up. No. I have to be the one to burn it. I'm meant to be the sacrifice. I have to drop it in the flame myself.

It's time to end this.

The Oldies start moving toward us, but I give a quick nod to Mike, and he clotheslines the two on the end, giving me enough space to run, quite literally, for my life. Mr. Brown is the first to chase me, but he still has my dad's leg, and I remember his weakness: zigzags.

I start sprinting up and down on Goodie Lane, forward and back, side to side, creating quick diagonals with my feet.

Brown doesn't stand a chance, and despite the efforts of the others, their stitched-up arms can't reach me. It's like every bit of training I've ever done. Every double-running session, every run with Mike, every race with Jess, every sprint with Dad: they've all led me to this moment. I don't stop until I make it to the grill.

"That's my girl," Grandma Jane says.

I don't hesitate. I drop the severed hand onto the flames, jumping back as the fire doubles in size.

Bea and the Oldies let out a scream so loud that I'm sure the rest of South Haven can hear it at the beach over the fireworks.

"You witch!" she howls to Grandma Jane.

"Takes one to know one," Grandma Jane replies.

The Oldies fall to their knees, an orange glow emanating from within each of them. Their makeup slowly starts to melt down, oozing into a puddle on the pavement, revealing not scars but thick, black stitches. One by one, the threads pop and burst, unbinding the Oldies' sewn-up bodies. What's left of their skin crinkles like paper, their bones visible beneath the aging surface. Their eyes roll back into their skulls and disappear, making them look like the skeletons I saw in their windows so many weeks ago. Their hair falls out in chunks around their now-frail, alien-like bodies. The orange glow grows stronger, brighter, more intense, and it is in this moment that I understand what's about to happen.

"Fire," I whisper.

Grandma Jane is now at my side, a protective arm around my shoulders. She smells like lighter fluid and chocolate cake and rosemary oil.

"Let this be a lesson to you, Beatrice," she calls out. "Age gracefully!"

With this, Bea lets out one last terrifying screech of fury as she and the rest of the Oldies burst into flames. I bury my face in Grandma Jane's arms and she pats my back, telling me it's OK to look. When I open my eyes again, all that remains is ash.

Mike steps in front of me. There are tears in his eyes. "I'm so sorry . . ."

I lunge forward and hug him. I feel his arms wrap around me and squeeze, and we stand there like this until Red speaks.

"Go inside," he says quietly to all of us. "I'll take care of this mess."

"Come on, kiddos," Grandma Jane says. She unlocks the front door and ushers us inside. "I think I've got some banana bread with your names on it." She turns toward Red and winks at him. "Please do join us when you're finished. What's your name, again?"

Red takes off his hat and bows cordially to Grandma Jane. "Red, ma'am."

Grandma Jane smiles. "My favorite color."

EPILOGUE

It's been two months since the Fourth of July. School doesn't start again for another three days, but I've been training with the eighth-grade track team for a few weeks now. I'm more than ready for a new year and a fresh start.

"You're late," I say, feeling someone behind me.

"Oh, man," Mike whines, jumping to my side. "I thought I'd get you."

"I don't scare so easily anymore," I tell him. "Whereas you"—I poke him in the chest—"are an even bigger scaredy-cat than you were before Operation Ghost Hunter."

Mike scoffs at me and lowers his Yankees hat. "Just run, Parker."

We take off toward Main Street, up the three side

streets, and around the cul-de-sac. I slow down when I see the pond.

"You know it's safe now, right?" Mike says. "We watched those Oldies burn. Now it's just a dirty old pond."

"I know," I say. Still, I can't get my feet to move forward. We stand in silence for a moment, staring at the murky water and the leaning lightning tree. I can't help but hold my breath as a ripple breaks through the surface. Did Sarah Goodie disappear when her daughter was vanquished? Or does she still lurk beneath?

Mike nudges me in the arm. "Let's just go around the other way."

I exhale. "Sounds good to me."

Together we cut through the opposite direction, ending up on the far end of Goodie Lane. Since Independence Day, it's been quieter. Rumor has it that the Oldies cut out to avoid taxes, or left abruptly to visit sick relatives, or ventured out to live in Mexico. Uncle Jack and some of the other officers did a quick investigation, but they didn't discover anything that raised eyebrows, which I'm sure is thanks to Ms. Attwood's cover-ups at the Town Hall. I don't know what happened to all of the Oldies' stuff, but apparently by the time the cops swooped in, everything was gone. Last week, all four houses went up for sale, one by one.

"Seems weird, doesn't it?" I ask, bending over to catch

my breath in the street. "For someone to sell the houses? I mean, how do they know the Oldies are gone for good?"

"Who cares," Mike says. "At least *we* know they're gone for good. Thanks to *you*." He grins at me. I grin back.

"Hi, honey," Grandma Jane calls, waving wildly from across the street. "I'm learning to garden. Can you believe it?" I give her a thumbs-up.

"They've gotten close, huh?" Mike says. He nods over toward Red's house, where Grandma Jane is knee-deep in a row of tomato plants. Red looks on lovingly from the side, giving her polite instructions on what to do, which parts to water, what leaves to pluck.

"Yeah, I think they like each other," I reply with a smile.

A loud horn suddenly blares behind us, edging us onto the sidewalk. Four large moving trucks barrel down the street, parking in front of the vacant houses. We stop in our tracks to stare.

"They sold already?" Mike asks in disbelief. "But how?"

"I told you something's strange about those for-sale signs."

The drivers hop out of the trucks and make their way to the back hatches. They silently begin to unpack furniture and arrange it on the four front lawns. Most everything is white, all antiques, all incredibly ornate.

"Who *are* these people?" Mike whispers.

At his words, four town cars roll onto Goodie Lane. One

parks in each driveway. A single woman gets out of each car, looking more like an old Hollywood movie star with each step. They give simple nods to one another before inspecting their furniture. Three of the women make their way into their new homes without a single word to each other or the movers, but the fourth woman stops at the edge of her lawn. Lowering her sunglasses, she looks straight at me with a devilish wink. I suddenly feel cold all over.

"You OK, Parker?" Mike asks, rubbing my arms. "You're freezing."

"Come on," I say quickly, forcing my eyes away from the woman in white. I pick up my pace. "Grandma Jane left us some banana bread."

We continue to move along the sidewalk, and when I look back, the woman is gone.

ACKNOWLEDGMENTS

The book you're holding was a dream come true to make, and it wouldn't exist without my dear family and friends, or my coven of experts.

First, thank you to my home team: Chris, Ruby, and Leo. Thank you for sparking this and so many other stories and for making me a better human. Special thanks to my mom for always being my number one cheerleader and for reading everything I've ever written since I was six years old.

Thank you to my family: Megan, Kaylee, Zoe, and Lex; the Venerusos and "the Haydens," especially Sal, for getting excited about early drafts and telling me to keep going. Thanks also to my English family: Janice, David, Jon, and Philippa. And of course, to my brother DJ, thanks for being my partner in crime growing up and for always watching spooky things with me even though you pretend to hate Halloween.

To all of my friends for the support and laughs throughout the years, especially the Hurds and the Kopanskis.

To my MG Squad: Janae Marks, Shannon Doleski, and Tanya Guerrero. And to Julie Dao, who saw something in this book before anyone else did.

I need to also thank my former teachers, especially

Michael Drout and Charlotte Meehan. And to my fellow teachers at BMS: I couldn't work with a better crew.

Thank you to my students for making me love my job.

To my agents past and present: Amy Tipton, for believing in this book and finding it a home, and Kathleen Rushall, for giving the soundest advice and enthusiasm—I can't wait to write many more stories with you at my side.

A million thanks to everyone at Abrams Books, especially Amy Vreeland, Jenn Jimenez, Megan Evans, Hallie Patterson, Patricia McNamara O'Neill, and Jenny Choy. Huge shout-out to Jean Hartig, Rob Sternitzky, and Penelope Cray for the keenest copyediting and proofreading eyes around. Thanks of course go to Marcie Lawrence, Gilles Ketting, and David Coulson for designing the amazing pages and cover art. And a very special thanks to my editors, Maggie Lehrman and Emily Daluga. My book couldn't have fallen into more competent, passionate hands. You have taken my baby and brought it to life. Not only have you made my dream come true, but you've also made me a better writer. I'm forever grateful.

And of course, thanks to you, my reader. I hope I scared the wits out of you.